PRAIRIE
SONGS

PAM CONRAD

PRAIRIE SONGS

illustrations by Darryl S. Zudeck

A Harper Trophy Book
Harper & Row, Publishers

I'd like to thank the Society of Children's Book Writers
for their Works-in-Progress Grant.

I also want to thank the people in Nebraska
who opened their offices and archives to me:
Anne Billsbach at the Willa Cather Museum;
Robert Manley at the Stuhr Museum of the Prairie Pioneer;
John Carter at the Historical Society in Lincoln;
and Roger L. Welsch, who showed me the way to Loup River—
even though I wouldn't sample his roasted goat.

Library of Congress Cataloging in Publication Data
Conrad, Pam.
   Prairie songs.

   Summary: Louisa's life in a loving pioneer family on
the Nebraska prairie is altered by the arrival of a new
doctor and his beautiful, tragically frail wife.
   [1. Frontier and pioneer life—Fiction.   2. Nebraska
—Fiction.   3. Family life—Fiction]   I. Zudeck,
Darryl S., ill.   II .Title.
PZ7.C76476Pr 1985   [Fic]   85-42633
ISBN 0-06-021336-1
ISBN 0-06-021337-X (lib. bdg.)

   (A Harper Trophy book)
ISBN 0-06-440206-1 (pbk.)

First Harper Trophy edition, 1987.

For H. D. Holoun,

who showed me his grandfather's old weathered soddy,

and for Mary Holoun,

who told me about the women

PRAIRIE SONGS

Chapter One

The prairie was like a giant plate, stretching all the way to the sky at the edges. And we were like two tiny peas left over from dinner, Lester and me. We couldn't even see the soddy from out there—just nothing, nothing in a big circle all around us. We still had Cap then, and he stood very still, shaking his harness now and again while we did our work, throwing cow chips into the back of the wagon, me singing all the while.

"Buffalo chips, buffalo chips, won't you marry me? Oh, come on out, buffalo chips, and dance all night by the sea."

Lester smiled and kept up a complicated clicking sound with his tongue and throat.

"Come on, Lester," I told him. "Sing! Nobody can hear ya out here. Oh, buffalo chips, buffalo chips," I sang louder and louder. "Come on, Lester."

But he just shook his head and even stopped his noises.

"Ah, you're no fun at all, Lester," I said, tossing a paddy of hardened dung into the wagon. I stood glaring at him, my hands on my hips, and tried to bully him. "You know something, if you practice talking and singing with me, and pretend I'm someone else, you might be able to really talk to strangers one day. You know that, Lester? Are you listenin' to me, Lester?"

Lester just smiled. "Leave me alone, prairie dog," he said. "Momma says leave off about that. It's none of your trouble."

None of my trouble, ha! He would never talk, and then I'd have to do all the talking. It was always up to me to answer questions that anyone would ask. I used to think I'd try not talking, too, like Lester. I clamped my mouth shut and folded my arms across my thin, bony chest. But it was too hard, and too hot to keep all those words inside with that sun beating down on me like hard rain.

"Come on, Lester," I said, breaking my silence. "Let's take a short rest before we start back." I got down on my hands and knees and crept beneath the wagon, the only patch of shade for miles and miles. Lester kept on tossing chips into the wagon, and with each thud the wagon would shake a thin sprinkling of dust on my face.

"Lester! I said, have a rest! I don't like dung dust in my hair!"

The tossing stopped, but I could see the backs of his brown dusty ankles standing slightly apart, very still.

"What are you doin' now, Lester? Would you get under here, please."

"I'm lookin'."

"What for?"

"The doctor and his wife."

I had forgotten all about that, and from my low place in the prairie grass, I looked around, through the wheels, between Cap's hooves, and saw nothing. "Which direction do you think they'll be comin' from?"

Lester dropped down and peered in at me. "New York is east, prairie dog."

"Lester," I said, with teeth-gritting patience, "they are comin' by railroad to Union Pacific Depot at Grand Island. And Grand Island is south, isn't it?"

"Oh." Lester sat down and leaned back against the wheel of the wagon, facing south. "What'll they be like?" he asked.

"Momma says they're probably very refined, and I heard Mrs. Whitfield say that they probably won't make it through the winter."

I stretched some prairie grass between my fingers and blew on it, making a high piercing whistle.

"Won't make it? Why?" Lester was looking at me, his eyes wide and troubled under his straw-colored hair.

"I don't know. I don't think people from back East are very strong, like we are. I think it's hard for them out here—the cold, the hot, the wind, the snakes. They're weak."

"You mean like Delilah?" His voice was soft.

"Yeah, like Delilah, I guess." I thought about our baby sister then, her round flushed cheeks and her blue eyes like store-bought marbles. "Remember how she used to finish her oatmeal and throw the bowl and yell 'all gone'?"

"Yep." Lester smiled and turned his face away. "You think the doctor and his wife will die, like Delilah?"

"Maybe," I told him. "Either die or go back East."

Lester was quiet. The prairie rang with silence, and Cap snorted and pawed the ground.

"Come on," I said. "I'm hungry. Let's go back."

We mounted the wagon and turned it around to face our house, or all we could see of it from that distance, the red flower of a windmill, beckoning us home.

Cap plodded on, rhythmically and slowly, and when Lester spotted some more chips, he jumped down from the front board. He gathered them up and sailed those pancakes into the back.

"Oh, darn! I never picked any flowers." I gazed off to the east where a thin mist of purple tinted the prairie grass. "Don't you think it would be nice to have flowers for the doctor and his wife when they come?"

Lester jumped up beside me. "Momma says get right back."

"Well, what difference does it make if we stop for a minute just to get some flowers? I think it would be nice. I think maybe they would like the prairie better if they could see the flowers."

Lester frowned. "I don't want to."

" 'Fraid of snakes?" I taunted, watching him out of the corner of my eye. "You know, there are snakes out by the chips, too, just like there are snakes by the flowers."

"Never seen any by the chips," he answered. "Just that time by the flowers. Maybe snakes like flowers."

"Oh, they're all over, Lester, even the one that was in the house that time."

He crossed his arms and thrust out his bottom lip as I slowed the wagon and turned it to face the field of flowers. "No," he said. "Momma says get right back."

"Are you scared?" I asked.

No answer.

"Lester Downing, you are one big baby." And of course,

at that, Lester's face became stone, and he wouldn't say another word.

I turned the wagon back again toward the windmill, and Cap turned his big shiny brown eye on me, as if to scold me and tell me to make up my mind. "Giddap, you old fool," I told him.

As we approached the windmill, the sod house itself began to rise up out of the hollow in the prairie, and we heard the bell ringing. Momma suddenly appeared around the side and began waving her white apron in the air.

"What's Momma doin'?" I asked Lester, squinting off into the brightness.

Her voice carried to us faintly, but the words were lost. "What is Momma *doin'*?" I asked again, and I slapped the reins to make Cap go faster.

As we drew closer to Momma, we could see she was pointing off to the south, and her voice became clearer. "Here they come!" she was calling. "Look!"

Lester silently pointed to a black dot on the horizon. Like the hands of Poppa's gold watch, it didn't seem to move, but as we watched we could detect a slight drift to what we knew would be Mr. Whitfield's wagon with Poppa, Mr. Whitfield and the doctor and his wife.

We rode up to Momma, who was smiling and excited. "Come on, Momma," I yelled. "Let's go right to the house. Let's meet them." I could barely sit still, and Lester, knowing he'd be meeting new people, slid off the wagon seat into the pile of dry chips.

"We have time, Louisa," Momma said. "Help me un-load the wagon first. We can hardly go call on the new doctor with a pile of chips in our wagon."

"But Momma—"

"Down, child. Get the sacks, and we'll have plenty of time. Lester, come." She held up her hands to Lester, and he leaped out of the wagon. "Get the sacks."

Once we had loaded the gunnysacks with the chips and had piled them against the wall in the sod stable, Momma carefully placed two linen-covered dishes on the back of the wagon, one containing bright-yellow cornmeal cakes and the other sweet butter. A large jar, screwed tightly shut, sloshed with fresh milk. Momma told Lester to sit in the back and make sure nothing spilled or slipped around, and she and I sat up in the front of the wagon and started off. The dot on the horizon seemed bigger, closer, and now no longer a dot but an undefined moving form traveling not toward us but in the direction of the doctor's house.

"I want to take them flowers, Momma. Just think how nice flowers would be when they get here. Please." I slipped my hand under her arm and looked up at her. "Please stop by the flowers."

Momma looked at me, in my eyes and all around my face. "Why, Louisa, for an instant you looked just like your grandmother. I swear. Like a look from my own momma delivered on your face."

That used to happen every so often, and so of course, when we arrived at the new sod house built especially for the doctor and his wife, I was carrying a small but beautiful bouquet of prairie flowers.

We stood waiting in front of the soddy, watching the distant wagon approach, and we were joined by our only neighbors, Mrs. Whitfield and her boy, Paulie, who had both come on foot.

Paulie was my age, and I hated him. I wouldn't even look at him but couldn't help hear him spit loud and far behind my back. Mrs. Whitfield squeezed Momma's hand and said in that loud, prayerful voice of hers, "Thank God, Clara. Praise the Lord."

Then as the wagon came closer and closer, Poppa waved and Mr. Whitfield's laugh reached us almost before the sound of the horse's hooves. We stood motionless in the fierce sunlight, ready with our practiced smiles and greetings, eager to welcome our new neighbors. But none of us waved and our smiles began to fade.

"My word, Momma," I whispered. "Look at that."

Lester forgot himself and stood up in the wagon. For there, in the back of the Whitfields' wagon, sat the doctor and his wife, but none of us even noticed the doctor. It was the wife.

There are two pictures of Emmeline Berryman I have frozen in my memory for all eternity, and this was the first. She was dressed in the most magnificent violet dress I could ever remember seeing, and across her lap lay a sparkling pink parasol flounced with lace and eyelet.

But she wasn't sitting up, ready and amused by our wide-eyed, droop-jawed welcoming party. She was slumped in a faint against the doctor, and her face was gray, like winter prairie grass before a bad storm.

Chapter Two

Momma was at the side of the wagon the moment it stopped, her hands gripping its edge. "J.T.," she said, looking up at Poppa, "what's wrong? Is she ill?" Her eyes went from Poppa to the doctor, and then to the small gray face pressed to his coat.

Poppa shrugged, and the doctor smiled slightly beneath the first fancy-trimmed mustache I had ever seen.

"Somewhat," the doctor answered. "A rather peculiar combination of too many trains, too many wagons and a new Berryman on the way.

"Emmeline, darling," he said, rubbing her arm gently and glancing at the welcoming party. "We're here. We're being greeted."

I couldn't take my eyes off that woman's face. Her head lifted slowly and her eyes seemed to remain unfocused. Her hair was bound up in two massive buns of braids, all colors and shades of yellow and brown. She was very gray, covered with a light sifting of train soot, but even so, she was more beautiful than anyone or anything I had ever seen.

We watched Mr. Whitfield leap heavily from the wagon and extend his hand to the doctor's wife. Without looking at him, she stood and then leaned into his arms. The swell of the unborn child was noticeable beneath the folds of her violet ruffles and, unexpectedly, the palest shoe showed beneath her hoops and she stepped lightly onto the dry grass.

The doctor jumped down and stood beside her, slipping an arm around her waist. Still she had not looked at anyone. I was spellbound. Lester had moved up behind me and was digging his chin into my shoulder.

Mr. Whitfield, who always liked giving speeches, cleared his throat and took off his hat. He twisted it nervously in his hands as he spoke. "Mr. and Mrs., uh, Dr. Berryman, on behalf of my family, the Whitfields, and our neighbor family here, the Downings, and on behalf of all the families and people of Howard County, we welcome you to the state of Nebraska. We welcome you." He looked nervously at his wife. "We like to think we're the best neighbors in any state of the union, and if there's anything you need, we want you to call on us. And now, in gratitude for your arrival, and as per our agreement, I present you with this fine soddy, built by me and J.T. here."

Dr. Berryman was smiling and looking from face to face at each of us. His clothes were dark and of some kind of fabric that didn't show its weave. He was handsome, like a man in one of Momma's magazine advertisements. Then Mrs. Berryman raised her head and looked at us. It was as if she were made of china, she was so pale and stiff.

"Thank you very much," the doctor said, in a voice smooth and soft. "I look forward to starting a new life here and I hope you'll not feel the need to treat me so formally. I am a doctor, and good at what I do, but neither my wife nor I know the first thing about living in Nebraska, and your skills are as valuable to me as mine are to you." His words seemed right with his fancy-trimmed mustache and his smooth clothes. Leaving his wife standing there, he approached us and shook hands with each of us, looking into our eyes and smiling.

I watched his wife as I would have watched a spinning top, waiting for her to fall over, and then I walked right up to her and held out the flowers that were a shade paler than her dress.

"Welcome to the prairie, ma'am. I hope you'll like it, and these here flowers are as good a place as any to start, and if you want me to show you where you can find them, I'd be glad to take you there, and we brought some corn cakes and butter, too, if you'd like some, and a little milk. . . ."

Emmeline Berryman reached out for the flowers and slipped her hand gently over mine, her fingers soft and cool. Her tongue flitted over her colorless lips. "Milk?" she asked. "I would certainly appreciate a glass of milk." Her hand remained on mine. I turned and looked at Momma.

"Ma?"

"Yes. Of course." Momma went quickly to the wagon and came back, balancing the plates and the jar. "Come inside, Mrs. Berryman," she said. "Sit yourself down and get comfortable. You're home now." Momma smiled warmly and led the way into the soddy. As she passed, I could see Lester clinging like a lizard to her skirts. Behind us, Paulie snorted, but Mrs. Berryman didn't seem to notice. She simply followed them into the house.

The soddy was dark and cool compared to the glaring heat and sun outside. At that time, it still had a new and welcoming feeling for me, and I stopped to let my eyes grow accustomed to the light. I could hear Momma putting the dishes on the table, and her funny double footsteps with Lester stuck to her. Then I could smell a wonderful lavender smell coming from Mrs. Berryman, and slowly all their dark forms came into focus.

"Ahh," said the doctor's wife. "How lovely and cool." She sank into the chair that my family had donated as part of their furnishings. Momma poured out a glass of milk and handed it to her.

"My name is Clara Downing," she said, slipping into the only other chair. "We live just three miles from here, over the western rise. We'll be close neighbors, if you should be needing."

Mrs. Berryman lowered her glass, leaving a childlike rim of white on her lips. She closed her eyes and sighed. "How do you do, Mrs. Downing. I apologize for my condition. I'm afraid I'm being very rude."

"Oh, no, not at all. And please call me Clara. Formalities are as useless as streetcar tracks out here."

She laughed, like a wind chime. "Hmm. I noticed. And please call me Emmeline."

For the first time, then, her eyes seemed to really focus, and I followed her gaze to my mother, suddenly shocked by the contrast. Was Momma really that plain? Plain as a walnut? Her hair was wound up out of sight, holding none of the promise of those wheat-colored treasures pinned behind Mrs. Berryman's delicate ears. Momma's face seemed heavy, her skin creased into fine folds like the sleeves of her blouse rolled up over her elbows.

"And the flower bearer? Lover of prairies? What is your name?"

She was talking to me. Momma looked at me expectantly. "Louisa Downing, ma'am, Emmeline, ma'am."

"Louisa!" Momma interrupted. "I think we could use a *few* formalities, even in this uncivilized wilderness, and one will be that you address your elders with a Mr. or a Mrs., please."

"Yes, Momma, Mrs. Berryman."

"And this?" Mrs. Berryman asked, bending forward slightly to see behind Momma. "Who might this be?"

"That's Lester," I answered. "He's my brother, and he only talks to the family. And even sometimes he don't talk none to us either, especially since Delilah died, but sometimes he talks to us, and sometimes he even sings a little, but mostly he's kind of shy."

Mrs. Berryman looked at Momma, who stood up suddenly and said, "You hardly give him a chance to answer for himself, Louisa, the way you go on."

At that moment Mr. Whitfield and Poppa carried a large black trunk into the soddy and placed it against the wall. Mrs. Whitfield and Paulie came in, too, and stood back against the walls like shadows.

"Whew, that's a heavy one," Poppa said.

Mrs. Berryman rose with a quiet shushing of her full skirts and extended her hand to him. "Thank you for your help, Mr. Downing. I'm afraid it's taken a glass of your wonderful milk to revive my good manners."

He seemed awkward to be offered a lady's hand, and for one awful instant I thought he might kiss it, but he just squeezed it gently and looked at Momma, plain Momma in her brown blouse.

"Books! Books! Books!" the doctor said, lugging in yet another box. He dropped it on the ground and wiped the perspiration off his face. "My, it's as cool as an icehouse in here."

Mrs. Whitfield ran her fingers over the trunk and then sat heavily on it. "I guess doctors need a lot of books for all their learnin'," she said. I knew she was just dying to look into those trunks, probably full of fine city things.

Dr. Berryman winked unexpectedly at me. "Ha! My doctoring books account for about two pounds of this wagonload. Most of those books are Emmeline's."

Emmeline's? Those books belonged to Mrs. Berryman? What kinds of books? Suddenly I was as anxious to look into those trunks as Mrs. Whitfield was.

"You exaggerate, William." His wife seemed to puff up like a small bird. She had begun to glow.

I watched with fascination as more and more boxes were brought in and deposited along the walls. We owned one book—an old Bible—and two magazines that were three years old, and sometimes the *Daily Independent* passed through our house. Momma had taught me a bit of reading, and I had read those pretty magazines so many times, I could have recited them right there, with them three miles away in my own soddy.

The room grew more and more crowded as the men piled the boxes up. I watched Mrs. Berryman stand and walk to the window. I knew what she would see, gazing out that way, through the deep window. Nothing. Clear, pure nothing for miles and miles. She stood there a long time, oblivious to the toting and shoving that was going on in the room. I watched as she moved her gaze from the window to the wall and slowly reached out a cautious finger to touch it.

"What is this?" she asked faintly. No one heard her but me. She turned and said louder, "What is this house made of?" Everyone was quiet. I saw her shiver.

Momma went to her side and patted the wall gingerly with her palm. "Sod," she said. "This is a good sod house, like ours. The sod is taken from the ground, made into strips, piled up like bricks, and built and shaped into a house. It's just like ours."

"You mean dirt? This is a dirt house?"

Momma seemed embarrassed. I watched her. I had always lived in a sod house. Momma had told me about other houses, houses built of wood, but all I could imagine were houses that looked like the insides of dresser drawers.

"It's not so bad, Emmeline," Momma told her. "See how cool it is? And in the winter it's as warm as a barn. And we can help you plaster the walls once the house has settled, if you like, once you're unpacked and—"

"And grow flowers on the roof," I added.

"And put down a rug on the ground," Momma said, smiling at me gratefully.

Mrs. Berryman looked down at her feet, at the dirt floor and then up at her husband. "We *will* have wooden floors, William, won't we?"

"Yes, dear, of course."

Poppa looked at the doctor. "Actually, there's no wood to be had, Doc."

Mrs. Berryman's face grew pinched and hard. "William, I thought we'd at least have a log cabin, isn't that what . . . what . . . pioneers usually have, log cabins?"

"Not in Nebraska," I told her. "No log cabins, no plank floors. Look." I stepped up close to her and pointed out the window. "For logs you need trees, for planks you need trees. Here we got brick houses, prairie brick."

Mrs. Berryman looked out through the window again. Her lavender smell filled me, and she said quietly, as if to herself, "There are no trees."

She looked at me then, set her glass on the table, and simply walked straight out the door. Everyone in the soddy looked at each other. Mrs. Whitfield pursed her lips and Momma folded her hands at her waist.

"William," came the call from outside.

The doctor stood with his thumb and forefinger pressing into his closed eyes. "Yes, dear. Excuse me," he murmured to us. He turned and walked out the door.

I ran to the doorway then, and Lester came to stand behind me. "Are they going to leave?" he whispered in my ear. We watched as they walked farther and farther from the house. When they were out of earshot, they turned and looked back at their soddy. I thought I saw Mrs. Berryman sway slightly, and then the doctor reached out and put his arm around her waist. They were beautiful out there, two figures in the sunlight of the summer prairie, a handsome doctor and his delicate wife, her violet dress shimmering like a flower field.

"Carney Whitfield!" Mrs. Whitfield growled at her husband. "Now you did it. A New York doctor! Ha! You are a crazy man, Carney. A doctor from Kansas City would have at least seen a soddy before." She stood and smoothed out her skirts fiercely. "I give them till midwinter, and they'll be looking for the first 'streetcar' out of here."

"Go easy, Pru," Momma said. "Go easy on them. They just got here, and they sure seem like good people. I remember how *I* felt when I first came." Momma hugged herself as if she were cold.

"And besides," I added, "she smells wonderful."

"Humpf! A lot of good *that* will do her—lavender, waxed mustaches, pleasure books. I never!" Mrs. Whitfield stared down at the boxes. "You mark my words, come spring they'll be gone like jackrabbits at the crack of a rifle."

"Well, J.T., let's go home," Momma said. "We can

come back tomorrow, once they're a little settled in."

"But Momma," I said. "The books! I want to see all the books!"

"Ha!" Mrs. Whitfield pulled herself up straight and rigid. "No book you need but the good Bible, Louisa Downing. Probably all kinds of frivolous things in there." She looked again at the boxes. "Lace curtains, silver napkin holders, poetry . . ."

"Come along, Louisa." Momma pushed her chair under the board table. "We'll see the books tomorrow. Get in the wagon."

"Git off, Lester!" I said suddenly, shaking him off my back. "Is that all you do, is hang?"

He bolted out the door and dove into the back of the wagon. If only we could have waited a few more minutes, I was sure they'd come back to the soddy and begin unpacking, stacking the books on the table—letters, words, pages and pages of magical paper. But Momma was behind me, nudging me out the door.

"Good day, Pru. Maybe we'll see you tomorrow," she said, pushing me some more.

We got in the wagon, Momma and Poppa on the bench, and Lester and me in the back. But Poppa sat very still. "Maybe I should tell them we'll be back tomorrow," he said to Momma, as if asking her.

Momma squinted off in the direction of the Berrymans. "That might be good, J.T."

We watched as Poppa walked off, his long legs moving slowly and easily through the grass. His hands were deep in his overall pockets and his shoulders were stooped over some. He spoke to them a minute, and he and the doctor shook hands. A sound of a man's laughter floated back to us, not Poppa's.

"That sure is one beautiful dress, isn't it, Momma?"

Momma looked back sharply, and for an instant I thought she might scold me. But she just turned her back. "That it is, Louisa, that it is."

Poppa returned, nodded to Momma and started Cap on back to our soddy. Lester and me sat with our feet dangling out the back. We watched the Berryman soddy disappear behind the rise, and then the small violet figure vanished as well. Momma and Poppa were silent and our shadows were monstrously long as night approached. I watched the spiderlike shadows of the wheels turning.

"Well, what do you think?" I asked Lester.

A bird whisked past us, giving off a shrill little call, and Lester whistled after it as it disappeared from sight. I thought he wasn't going to answer me, but after a while he shrugged.

"Mrs. Berryman is pretty," he said. "I hope they make it."

"They will," I answered. "He's a doctor, isn't he? Momma?"

"Yes?"

"Mrs. Berryman . . . she's going to have a baby?"

"That's right."

"See that, Lester? That'll be good."

"Why?" Lester looked puzzled. "What's so good about that?"

"A prairie baby. Then she'll have prairie flowers, a good soddy and a prairie baby. That'll make them happy."

Momma smiled back at me, but I knew even then it was a sad smile, and I felt drawn to her. I crawled across the wagon bed to where she and Poppa were and leaned my elbows on the board between them.

"Momma?"

"Mmm?"

"What's potery?"

"Poetry," she corrected, and looked up at Poppa. "J.T., how would you describe poetry?"

"Oh, maybe a song without the music."

That didn't satisfy me, but I was still, and then Poppa began quietly.

> *"Western wind, when wilt thou blow,*
> *The small rain down can rain?"*

"How nice, Poppa!" I knelt up high to see his face, and he continued.

> *"Christ, if my love were in my arms,*
> *And I in my bed again!"*

"Poppa!"

"James Thomas! Wherever did you pick that up?"

"Say it again, Poppa, say it again," begged Lester.

"He will not," Momma ordered. "Heavens, J.T., don't let Pru Whitfield hear you reciting stuff like that!"

Our still windmill rose over the swell, like a prairie dog peeking at us, and slowly our soddy grew up beside it. Our soddy with the flour-sack curtains, the flowers on the roof and the two magazines under my cot.

Chapter Three

Poppa and Dr. Berryman made a plan to go to Grand Island for supplies soon after that, and Momma arranged for the rest of us—her, Lester, Mrs. Berryman and me—to go on a picnic. She planned it as a nice outing, but I heard her tell Poppa how it would be a way to introduce Emmeline to cow chips and the need to be collecting them. The Berrymans didn't have a stove, which was one of the reasons for the trip to Grand

Island, but the days were as hot as blazes, so they really hadn't had call to burn anything yet.

I was excited about going on a picnic, because Momma hadn't kept her promise—we had not gone back the next day to see all the books. Momma and Poppa had each gone over, but never with me or Lester.

"They need to get used to things," Momma had said. "They don't need any nosy children poking around their belongings." But now Momma and Lester and me were walking along the wagon ruts to the Berrymans'. Lester and me were taking turns pushing each other in the wheelbarrow. Of course, I always got the shortest ride, and Lester even tipped me out a number of times, but seeing as how Poppa took the wagon, it was the only thing we had for picking chips.

"Look at you," Momma scolded. "Your hands are filthy dirty. And you want to see all Mrs. Berryman's books? Don't you touch a thing now, Louisa."

"But Momma, I'll wash up. Please, Momma. I've been waiting for three days to see those books."

Momma turned her back on us and kept on walking. She had been edgy that morning back at the soddy, combing her hair twice, peering into the cloudy reflection of the old tinned mirror, and putting on a fresh white apron that she usually used only for special occasions.

"Momma? You're wearing your good apron to go chip pickin'?" I had asked.

"That's right, Louisa."

"But Momma, it will be ruined."

"Louisa, wash your face," she had answered. "And your feet, too. I do declare, you two look like savages."

"But Momma, we're only goin' chip pickin'!"

I had the feeling Momma realized she looked like an old walnut next to Mrs. Berryman, so I kept complaining about having to wash at all, hoping she would say something about the difference between us and city folk. But she had said nothing as she jammed things into the food basket.

"Lester, get in this barrow now and be still," I told him. Momma had gotten way ahead. "Momma, hold up."

She stopped and looked back at us and beyond to our soddy, then around at the horizon. "Lord, it's hot today. And not a wisp of a cloud to be seen."

"Momma, does Poppa think you're pretty?"

Her eyes shot me through and through. "I don't rightly know. He ain't mentioned it lately."

"But did he *use* to think you were pretty?"

"Louisa, what's this about?"

"Can you imagine what it's like to be pretty like Mrs. Berryman? To have skin like that, and ears, and such smooth fingers?"

"No, I don't think I can imagine such a thing."

"It must be wonderful." I sighed.

"It ain't everything, you know. It's just another quality, that's all. A person can be pretty, or strong, or willful, or dependable, or caring, or loving. Seems to me I'd have a list of other things to be before I'd choose pretty."

My arms ached from holding up the wheelbarrow handles at my sides. "Git out, Lester. Lighten my load awhile."

"She's kind of pretty like Delilah, isn't she?" he asked, running up alongside Momma and slipping his hand in hers.

"What do you mean, Lester?" She reached out and tucked his hair behind his ears, and then stopped, spit on her fingers and smoothed down his cowlick.

"If you pick pretty, does that mean you can't pick strong?"

"Dear Lord, you children come up with the strangest notions. Come on. Keep walking here."

We could see Mrs. Berryman as soon as we saw the soddy, because she was outside, walking around the foundation. Once in a while she would stoop down to look at something and then disappear behind the house once more. When she saw us, she waved, and we heard her faint "Yoo-hoo!"

I was surprised she wasn't in violet anymore, as if she would always be. She was wearing a pale-blue gingham dress with a dark-blue apron tied high over her bulging middle. She began walking to meet us, her skirts swaying around her feet.

"Good morning, Emmeline," Momma said, letting go of Lester's hand and waving. Lester stepped behind her and peeked out from behind her skirts, keeping in step.

"Good morning, Clara. It's a beautiful day. A bit hot, but beautiful all the same, don't you think?"

Her face glistened with perspiration, and she touched her fingers to her splotched cheek. "Clara, you must tell me how to plant a garden," she said breathlessly. "You know, back home in New York, I had a lovely flower garden, and I've even brought some seeds, but I don't know the first thing about vegetables or fruit." She slipped her arm casually in Momma's arm and walked with us.

"Good morning, Louisa, Lester." She smiled over her shoulder. It seemed to me as if she had already adjusted to her dirt house.

"Your children are lovely, Clara. They are so lucky to grow up here, in nature, in the wild." She held out her arms to take in the prairie. "Do you know that in New York City they have a problem with packs of wild children roaming the streets? Imagine that. Stealing, robbing. Never saw it for myself, but I read about it." She stopped short and stared off toward the south. "I do hope William brings a newspaper back with him. I haven't had the chance to read any news in four weeks."

"But you have so many books, Mrs. Berryman," I said. I saw my chance.

She turned around and walked backward. She smiled at me, as graceful as a magazine lady in a hat advertisement. A straw bonnet with a long yellow streamer covered her head.

"Do you read, Louisa?"

"Some," I told her.

The inside of the soddy was cool, as I had remembered it. I had been in it many times before, while it was being built. Even before the rafters and the willow roof had been laid on. Now there were pink curtains over the windows, tacked into the not-yet-plastered sod. There was a table-cloth over the makeshift table and an intricate coverlet of pale-yellow crochet over the bed.

"You've made this feel like a real home, Emmeline," Momma told her.

She looked around and flapped her arms at her sides. "Oh? Do you think so? I don't think it looks like home. Don't think it ever will, to tell you the truth."

"What was it like in New York, Mrs. Berryman?" I eyed the rows of books lined up on top of and inside the cartons.

"Oh, it was lovely. There were moldings around the doors and windows carved with leaves and flowers, and there were gaslights hanging in every room, a bathroom with a porcelain sink and toilet, and there was a huge bathtub with water that came right out of it. And on the streets there were fruit wagons with fresh fruits and vegetables delivered every day right up the block."

Momma had a peculiar look on her face, kind of a held smile. "Whyever did you want to come here, Emmeline?

Seems you liked New York so, to hear you talk about it."

Mrs. Berryman shrugged and fingered the hem of her apron. "William" was all she said. Her hands passed lightly over the swell beneath her apron.

"So! Where is this picnic today? And what's this about cow . . . droppings?"

"Well, we thought we'd go walk out to the river, have a picnic, and then help you get your first load of cow chips. It's what we burn around here . . . because of not having any wood."

Mrs. Berryman looked at Momma blankly. "You burn cow manure?"

Momma began to stammer. "Well, when they're, um, old, and they're dry, and they really don't smell too much anymore . . ."

"Should I bring gloves?" Mrs. Berryman asked.

"Well, we'll eat first," Momma answered. "So it's up to you."

Mrs. Berryman opened her trunk and bent over it, digging into wads and depths of fabric to come up with a pair of dark-green gloves the color of moss.

"My goodness, I guess I have always taken coal and wood seriously for granted." She stood up sharply and eyed us. "No one builds *houses* of cow chips, do they?"

Lester laughed. I can't remember him ever doing that before then, laughing outright in front of a stranger. Mrs. Berryman blushed a deep red and slipped the gloves onto her hands. "This should do me." She wiggled her fingers at Lester and flounced out the door. We followed, and I was keenly aware that I had still not gotten a chance to look at those books, not a single one.

We all walked down to the Loup River, leaving the wheelbarrow on the high ground for later. We cut through a stand of old cottonwoods and high grasses, and the river opened wide before us. Even from a distance we could see it moving along, shallow and swift.

Momma persuaded Emmeline to take off her shoes and stockings, and then we walked out through the swampy bright-green water till we got to a broad bar of dry sand.

Momma spread the coverlet on the hard ground and put out the eggs and cheeses, a loaf of bread, a bowl of strawberries and a small loaf of gingerbread. There was a jar of dark coffee that she and Mrs. Berryman shared as they talked. Lester and me drank buttermilk and listened, digging our toes into the crusts of sand.

"But one day," Momma was saying, "shortly after that, J.T. and I were sitting around the table, and the children were just rousing themselves up, when in walks two of them, bold as you please." Momma cupped her hand over her small breast. "I can tell you, Emmeline, I thought it was all over." But she laughed. "There they were in beads and skins, and this bright, rich-colored red skin, like . . . like . . . I don't know . . . autumn apples. Maybe if it had been two men I would have been really frightened, but it was a man and a woman, and she had a baby strapped to her back."

Mrs. Berryman's eyes were as big as eggs, and she nervously tucked her skirt around her feet as she sat there.

"Well"—Momma's voice dipped—"we had Delilah at the time, and she was in my lap suckling, and J.T. says to me, 'Be calm, Clara, just be calm as can be.' Well, I'm sure my milk just stopped that instant like a spigot shut off. But I sat there, and Delilah, well, she was kind of dozing off."

Momma looked off into the distance, and I felt all squirmy, wanting her to go on and not start thinking about Delilah.

"And?" Mrs. Berryman sat frozen with a hard-cooked egg in her hand.

"Yes, and the woman, she came over to me, and reached out this wide dark finger and touched Delilah's cheek."

I felt Mrs. Berryman shiver beside me.

"She smiled and said something, but I couldn't understand her, and she turned a little so I could see her baby. He had these big black eyes, as cute as can be, looking out at me. And then the man began walking around the soddy, looking here and there at everything. Well, here I am wondering if he's going to take our things or hurt us, and Lester and Louisa just rousing out of their sleep. I can tell you, Emmeline, I was plenty scared."

Momma took a long sip of her coffee, and I watched as Emmeline brought a trembling cup up to her own lips. "And then, Clara?"

Momma started to chuckle, real deep, and I knew the rest of the story, and I could have told it along with her, I had heard it told and retold so many times.

"It's honestly the one time I can say that Jesus Christ himself saved our lives. Here's this dark animal-smelling Indian gentleman looking around at our things, and his wife sat down on the floor by my feet and pulls her own youngun to her breast and begins nursing. Like it was her own home. The man opened boxes, tapped spoons together like music, tasted our ground flour and chewed on some coffee beans, shook the kerosene lamp, which, thank goodness, was not lit, and then he comes upon the Bible sitting right where it still is now, on the shelf next to the stove. He picks it up and begins looking at it, holds it up real close to his nose, staring at the letters, and then he comes to the pictures. Like a little boy, he sat down next to the woman and showed her the picture of the Nativity. I could see, 'cause they were right by my feet. Whew, they smelled like two dogs who'd been out in the rain. They're smiling and touching the picture, and then they turn to the picture of Noah herding the animals onto the ark. The woman took the book into her own hands then, and touched it and rubbed it, and then she turned the page, and what should she come to but the picture of Jesus nailed to the cross!"

At this point, Momma would always slap her hands down on her thighs for emphasis. She rocked back and grinned. "Those two savages looked at that picture for less time than it takes a mosquito to get you, and they were out the door and down the path, gone! Gone! Gone! Praise the Lord, as my old grandpa used to say." Momma sighed, satisfied with her story, puffed up with a story-teller's pride.

Mrs. Berryman looked horror-stricken. They looked at each other.

"Emmeline! What's the matter?"

"They didn't touch the children?"

"Why, no." Momma reached out and patted her hand reassuringly. "Oh, Emmeline, did I frighten you? It's nothing to worry about. You'll get used to it. Actually, that was the last we saw an Indian, and that must have been seven or eight months ago. There aren't many around anymore."

"Didn't Mr. Downing try to shoot them or frighten them away?"

"No, that wouldn't be good. They don't mean no harm. We haven't had any trouble around here to speak of. You have to learn to just be calm around them. They go away once they've satisfied their curiosity . . . or their appetites—that's all."

"William would shoot them, I'm sure."

"I hope not, Emmeline. Then more would come back. That's not the way to handle them."

There was silence then, and I had the keen sense that there was a bristling disagreement that was going on un-said, unfought, due to manners and the newness of friend-ships.

Mrs. Berryman wrung her hands and looked all around. "Maybe we should start back. I don't feel safe here. When will William and Mr. Downing return?"

"Oh, come, Emmeline, please. I'm sorry. I shouldn't have told you all that just yet. I didn't mean to frighten you. And it won't frighten you, either, after some time here. We are always careful, always cautious, but we're not afraid anymore, not like we used to be. There's some kind of hope and acceptance that replaces that fear. Soon there will be many more people out here—churches, schools, maybe even opera houses, good shops . . . and vegetable carts and streetcars. Right, Lester?" Momma pulled Lester onto her lap and ruffled his hair.

"Where is Delilah?" Mrs. Berryman asked abruptly, almost to hurt Momma, it seemed to me then.

"We lost Delilah," Momma said simply.

"Indians?"

"Oh, goodness, no! In November one night she began coughing and coughing, and there was just nothing to give her peace. She was so little, always little, and a bit too frail, I guess. Sweet like honey she was, though." Momma rested her chin on Lester's head. "We all miss her."

We sat quiet for a while, Momma rocking Lester, me braiding blades of grass, and Mrs. Berryman looking out for Nebraska savages. I do declare, she was a nervous lady, even then.

"Why, Emmeline, look at your apron!" Momma was suddenly smiling. Lester looked boldly with her. And there, beneath her apron, Mrs. Berryman's belly, like a puppy in a sack, shook and seemed to take a mighty shift. She laughed, easy and soft, smoothing her hands down over the ball of her unborn babe.

I was remembering how Delilah did that, before she was born, before we knew it was Delilah, when Mrs. Berryman reached out to me.

"Would you like to feel him kick, Louisa?" She placed my hand flat on her belly, and we waited. Our eyes held each other's in a playful grasp. She looked mischievous, naughty. "Come on, little fellow, give us a kick," she whispered. Stillness, just the smooth cotton of her dress. She knelt in the grass. "Lester, come. Maybe he will dance for you."

I was sure Lester wouldn't do it, but he did. Crawled to her on his knees, and she pressed his small hand to the other side. He stared at the front of my chest, as if he didn't know what he was doing, touching the taut belly of beautiful Mrs. Berryman, waiting for her little kitten to flop.

"Oh, I can't stand it." Momma laughed and she came over, too, and pressed her hand on the rise. We held very still, waiting while the river ran silently past, and the prairie lay all around us full of secrets, full of graves and promises that we might not want kept.

And the baby didn't move, not even a little.

Chapter Four

Lester and me hunted tadpoles that afternoon, and I picked a bouquet of beautiful wildflowers that I split down the middle and shared with Mrs. Berryman. I gave her the cattail.

Later we gathered chips and gave them all to her, to get them started. She wore those green gloves and handled the chips as if they were hot, burning her clear to the

bone. And we even helped her stack them up, and then we pushed the wheelbarrow home, empty again.

I was furious at Momma. Never once did she mention the books, and we never went inside again, but stood outside the soddy for parting words. Mrs. Berryman was all the while looking for either her husband or Indians to come riding over the rim of the prairie.

I wouldn't even let Lester ride this time, I was so angry at Momma. "Momma, you promised. You promised. What if she goes back to New York and takes all her books, and I never get the chance to see them?"

"Patience, Louisa. I've invited Dr. and Mrs. Berryman for dinner in two days, and I have a plan, something better than just asking for you to browse through her books. Anyway, I seriously doubt they will go back to New York within the next week or so." Momma laughed. "She won't be traveling anymore with that little baby getting closer and closer to being born."

"What plan?"

"You'll see, Louisa, you'll see."

And as I set the table two days later for our dinner guests, Momma still hadn't told me.

She pushed the table up alongside the bed. "You and Lester sit on this side, Louisa, and use the tin dishes. And make sure you put the good forks alongside the china plates. You children take the crooked forks, and please, Louisa, try to remember some manners."

"Momma, you already told me. How come you don't tell Lester that? He needs manners, too, doesn't he?"

"I'm referring to the kind of manners that have to do with a busy mouth, Louisa Downing, which is something I don't worry about with Lester."

That hurt me. "I swear, sometimes I think you like Lester better because he don't talk—"

Momma pulled me to her suddenly, but I held myself real rigid. "Louisa, Louisa. That's not true. You know how I worry about Lester, growing up out here, and being so withdrawn and quiet." She held my face firmly to her warm chest, rubbing my ear between her fingers. "I am ever grateful that you are such a talkative, lively child, out here with nothing to stimulate you."

"What's stimulate?"

"Oh, stimulate is to have fancy moldings, and lots of people, and music, and streets and signs and books and civilized things, but I have a plan, Louisa. A plan for you and Lester, something to help you both."

"Here they are!" yelled Lester from outside. He ran in, peered nervously through the window at the approaching wagon, and ran out again.

While in Grand Island with Poppa, Doc Berryman had bought himself a horse and a fine wagon, the most beautiful two-seater wagon, painted shiny black, that looked sort of silly behind the plain gray horse. As they got closer, the doctor made the horse trot faster, and Mrs. Berryman held on to her bonnet. "William! William!" We could hear her laughing.

"Good afternoon, good neighbors," Doc said, pulling up alongside the house. "I want you to know this is my first call in my splendid new vehicle, and I am glad to say it is on such pleasant business, and no one is sick or ailing." He reached out to touch Lester's head as he climbed down from the wagon, but Lester ducked him.

"Lester, darling," Mrs. Berryman said, slipping off her seat and peering under the wagon. "I have something for you." She held out her hand, and I saw Lester snatch something. "And Louisa." She turned to me and held out a little package wrapped in white paper.

"Thank you, ma'am."

To Momma she held out a bouquet of flowers, blue and purple, tied with a satin ribbon that was as pink as a newborn kitten's tongue. Momma led the doctor and Mrs. Berryman inside, and I stood there in the late-afternoon sun and unwrapped the small package. Inside the crinkly paper was a heart-shaped piece of white gum with a sticker pasted on it—a rosy-cheeked angel with curly hair. I sniffed it and a clear peppermint scent filled my head.

"Look," Lester whispered. He had one, too, but his sticker was a picture of a yellow bird. We stood staring at them. I popped it in my mouth, and it was sweeter than honey. "These must be what they eat in New York," he whispered, and his very words spun away from us in the warm breeze like a dry tumbleweed.

When we finally went inside, Mrs. Berryman was standing in the center of the room, staring straight up. "Oh, Clara, what a wonderful idea." There was a double length of muslin tacked to the ceiling, reflecting light and keeping the dirt from sprinkling down on us. "William, we must do that. Find out how Mr. Downing did it." She smiled sweetly at Poppa, who reddened.

"Well, actually," Poppa stammered, "I didn't do it. It was Clara. I'm sure she'd be glad to show you how." *I* could have shown her, too. We always helped Momma, Lester and me, with the ceiling cover when it was time to wash it. Then Momma would hammer the muslin up, spitting out dust as it rained down on her, and we would hold the ends and hand up nails to her, the dirt stinging our eyes.

We all sat around the tightly packed table as Momma passed the serving plates. Doc and Mrs. Berryman got the chairs, Lester and me sat on the bed, and Momma and Poppa sat on the two barrels, making Poppa especially tall. I peeked under the table to see his two feet on each side of the barrel. He winked at me and stooped over a little more.

"This dinner smells wonderful," Mrs. Berryman said, fingering the silverware by her plate. "I'm afraid I'm not a very good cook."

Doc patted her hand and smiled, not at her, but around at the rest of us. "She's a fine cook, just fine."

Momma held the bowl of green beans out to her and seemed to study her face. "Well, it may be a little different cooking out here without vegetable carts and a wide choice of things all the time, but you'll learn, Emmeline. We all do."

Mrs. Berryman's cheeks were once again splotched, and her delicate neck became mottled before my eyes. She slipped her hand out from under her husband's. "I don't know. I grew up in a house with servants, and a cook. It's hard for me."

Momma looked startled.

"Yes, Emmeline, dear," the doctor said, "but you *did* cook for a year when we were first married, before we came here. I think you managed quite well."

"Did you have slaves, Mrs. Berryman?" I asked, knowing something, but very little, about the nature of servants.

"No . . ." she began, but Doc cleared his throat and started talking loudly to Poppa.

"Carney Whitfield has agreed to take me on an expedition of the county to meet some of the people in the area, and to let them know my services are available. I thought I would start as soon as possible, while the weather is still in my favor."

Doc had turned from his wife and was directing himself to Poppa. The doc's mustache was as black and shiny as his new wagon, and his eyebrows were softer and stuck out from his brow. "I'm anxious to meet the people and set up some kind of system for my services."

Momma smoothed her skirts. "Oh, I'm sure they'll all be delighted to meet you. But be prepared to see the results of some mighty poor doctoring. They've all done without for a long time. They've been making do all on their own."

Poppa chuckled and bit off a piece of hard bread. He held up his small crooked finger in front of himself as if to admire it. "Oh, I don't know, Clara, you didn't do too bad for yourself."

Doc grabbed Poppa's finger and felt for the bone. "Your handiwork, Clara?"

Momma blushed. "In a pinch, Doc. In a pinch."

"I could rebreak it for you, J.T., and set it right, give you more use of it."

Poppa pulled back his hand. "I get plenty of use, that's for certain."

"Who knows if we would have lost Delilah if you'd been here sooner. I often think of that." Momma pushed the rice around her plate. And everyone grew quiet.

"Emmeline told me you lost your child, Clara. I'm sorry to hear it. Let's hope things will be better for you now." He seemed awfully proud to me, in a way I wasn't sure I liked.

"You mean nobody's gonna die anymore?"

It was Lester, and we all stared at him in surprise, except the doctor, who didn't realize that Lester never spoke to anyone like that. He sipped his coffee.

"That would be nice, son. That certainly would be a nice goal."

Momma laughed. "Imagine that! Nebraska, the state where nobody ever dies anymore. Goodness, would we have people settling in these parts! Like some kind of gold rush." And she ruffled Lester's hair playfully.

"I need to make another stop at Grand Island," the doctor went on, "and see if those medical supplies have arrived yet. We sent them separately. I hope they come soon."

"Things are slow around here," Poppa said. "Especially the mail, although sometimes it'll surprise you."

"Oh, I do hope the cradle gets here in time," Mrs. Berryman said. "My parents are having a cradle shipped out from New York. It was imported from Germany, and Mother says it's beautiful. She wouldn't let me look at it before I left. Said it was bad luck."

"We slept in drawers when we were babies," I announced.

Poppa smiled at me. "That's right. And when you were too noisy, I just shut the drawer. Said, 'Good night, little sparrow,' and away you went."

"Oh, dear, I guess a cradle is pretty frivolous for prairie life." Mrs. Berryman was looking at me.

"Not at all," Momma assured her. "I can't wait to see it."

When all the bowls were empty, Momma suggested we sit outside and eat our applesauce, made from apples imported from Philadelphia.

It was cooler out, and the sun was beginning to turn the sky a sweet apricot color. We set the chairs and barrels facing the sun, and ate our desserts sprinkled delicately with fine cinnamon. Doc pulled out a pipe from his pocket and stuffed it with tobacco. He offered Poppa his pouch, but Poppa refused. I knew he had a corncob pipe inside, but I also knew it was cracked.

"It's so peaceful," Momma sighed.

"So empty," Mrs. Berryman said. Her small bowl sat atop her belly, and she looked all around her. "Sometimes I think I see shadows moving, maybe Indians coming. Or thieves."

"Emmeline, Emmeline," scolded the doctor between puffs. "You have read too many adventure stories. There are no Indians out here anymore."

"There are," Poppa said thoughtfully. He cupped his two hands around the bowl and stared out at the horizon. "Nothing bad's ever happened to us, though. There aren't many left anymore, but once in a while they come and look around, and then they leave."

"I told you, William," Mrs. Berryman said, leaning

forward and looking into her husband's face. She sat back again and glared at the setting sun. "He doesn't believe me half the time."

"Clara," the doctor asked Momma abruptly, "are you armed?"

Momma half smiled. "Not at the moment."

"But do you keep a gun in the house?"

"Yes, there's a rifle. It's for hunting, and protection if we should ever need it."

"Do you know how to shoot it?"

"Yes." Momma waited.

"Maybe you could show Emmeline."

"William! I couldn't shoot a gun! I won't!"

Poppa set his empty bowl on the ground next to him and rubbed his hands thoughtfully on the rim of his seat. "That's not such a bad idea, Mrs. Berryman. Not that you'll need it, but just in case."

"There will be times when I'll be away for a few days, Emm, and I would feel better about you and the baby if I knew you were armed." His mustache twitched.

Mrs. Berryman visibly softened at the mention of the baby, as the doctor had probably known she would. She stood up and once again scanned the horizon as if she were expecting someone. "Oh, I don't know, William. I just don't know. It frightens me."

"Don't be such a child," he said sternly. I had never heard Poppa talk to Momma that way, and I guess I was staring in wide-eyed amazement, because Momma caught my eye and pursed her lips together as if she were about to warn me. But she stood up and said, "Come, Emmeline, and see my vegetable garden. It's doing so well this year. I can give you some fresh things to take home with you."

Mrs. Berryman seemed as grateful as I was to leave the quiet gathering in front of the soddy, and the man who scolded her so easily. Lester ran ahead.

Midway between the house and the river was a square of dark earth that Momma always fussed over, forcing it to bear its yearly crop of vegetables. She churned manure into the soil in the autumn, and lugged buckets of water up from the river or down from the well all spring and summer. A cloud of dust followed us down to the garden, and Lester disappeared into its bushes of tomatoes and spears of standing corn.

"I worry about the children out here," Momma was saying. "With it being so wild and uncultured and all." Mrs. Berryman was quiet, listening. "And I have thought up something." Momma stopped and faced the other woman, and then started on again, her steps as hesitant as the words she was searching for. "I know how hard it is for you to carry water now that you're so far along, and well, I thought . . . I was thinking that laundry might be difficult for you, and seeing as how we have a pump, I was wondering if . . . I'd like to suggest that maybe . . ."

I walked up beside Momma, watching my bare feet walk

along while my whole body seemed to be waiting ears.

"I'd be glad to do your laundry chores for you, in return for you teaching Louisa and Lester here a little reading and writing, and maybe some arithmetic, just so they don't grow up totally—"

Mrs. Berryman stopped suddenly. "I'm not a qualified teacher, Clara. Not at all."

"But you may be the best chance they ever have, Emmeline. There are no schools yet in this part of the country. You have books, and you could teach them, maybe just a couple of days a week." Momma reached out and touched Emmeline's arm. "And Lester. I'm so worried about him. He says so little. It's unnatural, his quietness. Maybe if he could read. And he seems to like you a bit."

I suddenly realized how hard it was for Momma to do this. I was torn between the joy of maybe having Mrs. Berryman teach me, and the shame of seeing my momma ask so hard for something. She looked like a walnut again. Mrs. Berryman stood there, fingering her delicate straw hat in her hands.

"I hadn't thought of ever doing anything like that." She looked back at her husband, his chair tilted against the light side of the house alongside Poppa. "But you know, it might be good for me as well, to have such important work to do." She smiled at me. "Would you like to go to my school, Louisa?"

"Oh, yes, ma'am. Yes, I would. And I would help you,

too. Tote clothes for you, and bring you butter, and help you tack your muslin overhead, and keep your books piled neat."

She and Momma laughed. "And you, Lester? What do you think?" Mrs. Berryman reached down to touch Lester's back as he knelt in the dirt by her feet. But he shot off like a jackrabbit before she could. In the dirt, though, he had scraped out the only word he knew how to write. A word Momma had taught him during the winter, when we were worried about the snow that was piled heavy on our roof. It said: Lester.

Chapter Five

Momma put the lid on the soup pot and patted her flushed face with her apron. "Sounds like Carney Whitfield wants to be running for office or something," she complained. "The way he's escorting Doc all over the county as if it were some sort of gift he fixed up himself for everyone."

"Better him than me, Clara," Poppa said. "If he wants

to spend his time doing that, that's his business. The corn'll come ripe real soon, and I got too much to do to be fooling around with that sort of thing."

"It's going to be hard on Emmeline for a while, that's for sure. She's not used to being alone."

"Well, neither were you, Clara, and you made out just fine. There were many times I had to be gone, and you did fine. So will she."

Momma sighed and hung her apron on the hook beside the table. "Yes, but she's not quite up to it. I don't think so. I get an uneasy feeling about her. She gets herself in such a dither about Indians and coyotes and snakes. I never." Momma turned to me. "Will you stay here, Louisa? Or are you coming? We'll just be down at the river."

"I'm coming."

She frowned. "I don't know. I think you'd better stay here."

"Momma, please. You can show *me* how to shoot, too."

She secured her muslin hat around her head and tied it with great concentration. "No, Louisa, if you come, you just stay down and be still. Is that clear?"

"Aw, Momma—"

"Then stay here."

The grass at the river was fine and soft. Lester lay beside me, carrying on. "Whoa!" he shouted. "Whoa!" He was spread-eagle on his back, his arms and legs open wide, and he was staring up at the sky. He was a perfect five-pointed star.

"Lester, what are you doing?"

"I'm falling. I feel like I'm falling through the sky!"

I got down beside him—actually, sort of above him—with my head touching his, and my arms and legs spread out in all directions, like his. I looked up at the sky with him. He was right. There was such a vastness to what I could see, just sky, as if someone had taken scissors and clipped away the earth and all signs of it.

"I feel something pushing me down," he said quietly. "Like a big soft hand."

I could feel it, too, a warm presence holding me to the ground, like thick binding holding an Indian baby to its mother's back.

"I'm the papoose of the earth," I announced grandly.

Lester's laugh was cut short by the clap of a rifle, and we sat up.

Emmeline Berryman stood poised on the grass, like a little china figurine, the rifle pressed into her shoulder. Her feet were set slightly apart, and she held her aim steadily on the pan that hung on the cottonwood tree.

A crack had seared the stillness of the day, but no ping had followed to tell us she had hit the mark. She lowered the rifle and rubbed her shoulder. "Oh, Clara, this is absurd. I will never be any good at this. I think I'll just be scalped or eaten alive or whatever. This is hopeless."

Momma took the rifle and cracked it in half. Even though she had never taught me, I was certain that from watching I would know exactly what to do.

"Watch, now," Momma said. Their heads bent over the rifle as Momma loaded it, clicked it shut and handed it back to Emmeline.

"Once more," Momma said, "and then I have to get back."

I closed one eye and aimed with her, the white tin spot hanging still in the sunlight. The shot rang out and a sharp ping followed. "That's it! That's it!" Mrs. Berryman shouted. She ran awkwardly to the tree, her hands pressed under her belly, and she examined the pan. "Not exactly a bull's-eye, but I did scrape the edge some."

Momma stood with her hands on her hips, shaking her head. "Well, I hope you don't ever have to use it, dear. Or if you do, I hope whoever or whatever you aim at is frightened enough to run before you have to demonstrate your skill."

"Oh, me." Emmeline sighed. "If I wave a rifle at a coyote, will he run?"

"No," Momma answered. "Just shoot. The noise will frighten him."

"And Indians? If I wave a rifle at an Indian, will he run?"

Momma took the rifle from her and cleaned it, easily and expertly, as she would wipe a child's face. "Well, it may be handy to let an Indian know you have a rifle at your side, but don't get careless, Emmeline. Cautious, but not careless. Don't do anything you'll regret."

Momma handed back her rifle, and Emmeline carried it awkwardly at her side. We started back through the dense growth of cottonwoods to the path that ran between our two soddies.

"When will William be leaving?" Momma asked. I noticed how she only called Doc Berryman William when she was talking alone to Emmeline.

"Tomorrow."

We walked quietly, Lester hanging back, then running ahead, trying to get me to chase him until Momma told him to stop. When we got to the wagon ruts, we paused.

"Thank you, Clara."

Momma smiled and smoothed down her apron.

"I'll see you." Emmeline started off alone in the direction of her soddy.

Suddenly a wagon appeared, coming over the hill, a peculiar boxed type of thing, maybe like a gypsy wagon I had once seen, but it was smaller, and plain, and there was but one lonely man sitting in the seat. The wagon moved slowly, despite the snap of the reins. The horse was either old or very tired. All four of us stood and watched it approach.

"Who's that, Momma?" I asked.

"No one I've ever seen before," she answered. Mrs.

Berryman held the rifle sideways beneath her belly and walked slowly back to us. I don't have to tell you where Lester was.

"Good afternoon, ladies." The man tipped his pale-gray hat to us. "And how are you this fine afternoon?" he asked, reining the horse to a halt. I began to think he might be a circus performer or a carnival act. He had smiling eyes and a block of a beard that covered the lower half of his face somewhat. He climbed down from his seat and extended his hand to me. "Solomon Butcher, ma'am. You must be the lady of the estate."

I couldn't help but laugh. His warm hand engulfed mine, and I noticed a sharp smell coming from him, like no smell I'd ever met up with before. "And these are your daughters?" He bowed to Momma and Mrs. Berryman. "How lovely."

Momma was smiling. "I'm afraid, sir, that *I* am the lady of the land you're on right now. Mrs. Downing. Pleased to meet you, and this is Mrs. Berryman, who lives over three miles or so."

He pretended confusion and stared at me. "Pardon me, then you must be the grandmother."

"This is Louisa, my daughter. Lester, my son." Lester didn't come out from behind her, so she just patted the arms that circled her waist from behind.

"Pleased to meet you," he said, suddenly solemn and serious. "I truly am. Every time I ride along and come across a family at work or at play, I am deeply moved by the sight." He had placed his hat over his heart, and his eyebrows danced up and down with his words. "You are pioneers of Nebraska, pilgrims of the New World."

I looked at Momma in time to see her exchange a skeptical glance with Mrs. Berryman. "And what can we do for you, Mr. Butcher? Are you just passing through, or have you business here?"

"Business," he said, as if he liked that word. He walked to the back of his wagon and opened the door of the enclosure. It hung crookedly on one hinge, and as I walked around after him I was hit with a stronger draft of that strange smell. "I am putting together a book, ladies, a book about courage and endurance." He turned gently and extended his arm to all of us. "A book about you."

Momma was silent.

"Us?" I asked.

He pulled out a stack of papers, shuffled through them quickly, and returned half to the smelly wagon and held out the other half to Momma. I peered over her arm as one by one she looked at the papers. They were like pages of a book, but stiff and shiny, and in the center of each one was a picture of a soddy, and before each soddy was a family—three, six, sometimes ten people, all serious and grim.

"Photographs," Mrs. Berryman said quietly. "They are family portraits."

"Oh, they're more than that, Mrs. Berryman. They are recorded history. As it happens. Preserved for all time, the faces and lives of the people of this county. Look." He pointed to a horse that stood beside a soddy in one of the photographs. "Look at the ribs on that animal. Hard times. Yes, indeed. Hard times. And they won't be forgotten now, not the faces, or the animals, or the rolling hills. Now that I've begun my scheme."

"And what exactly is that, Mr. Butcher?"

"My book," he announced proudly. "Which will be a combination of photographs and biographies of the people who live in this county."

I can tell you it wasn't long before Solomon Butcher had Momma, Poppa, Mrs. Berryman and me posing in front of our soddy. I helped Momma drag out the two chairs we had. She and Mrs. Berryman sat in them, and I stood behind Momma with my hand on her shoulder. Poppa stood next to her, tapping his hand on his thigh with impatience. Lester wouldn't come out of the soddy.

"Be very still now," Mr. Butcher warned. We watched as he worked in the back of his wagon, mixing solutions and smells, and then he ran from his wagon, snapped a piece of glass inside his three-legged camera, and ducked beneath a black cloth. He held up his hand, his face hidden behind the glass eye of the black box. "Hold it! Hold it!" There was a click and then he hurriedly removed the glass and ran back to the wagon and up inside it.

We sat very still and waited. "All right" came his muffled voice from the wagon. Poppa pushed his hat back on. "*Now* can I get back to work?"

I ran to the wagon and peered into the sharp-smelling darkness.

"Can I see, Mr. Butcher? Is it ready?"

"Oh, no, child. I have to take it back to my house and develop the photoprints there. These are just the negatives." He dipped the glass in and out of a dark fluid.

"You mean we won't get to see it?"

"Why, sure, you will. You'll get to buy the book with the picture in it. I may even have a little showing in town one day."

I was so disappointed. I looked back at the soddy and tried to imagine it frozen in a picture with all of us in it. A photograph of us. I couldn't believe it. Momma had pictures of people in her family, my grandmother, her brothers. I liked looking at them, finding brooches and cuffs and tricky eyes, but I couldn't imagine an actual photograph of me. I wondered what I would look like.

Chapter Six

Lester and me walked there in the warm morning sunshine, my cheeks still hot from Momma scrubbing me so hard, and the collar of my dress still wet. Lester was hanging on me and holding back something awful.

"Lester, I refuse to carry you. Either you're going or you ain't going, but I'm not gonna pull you there, is that clear?"

"What'll she make me do, Louisa? What's gonna happen?"

"She's gonna teach us to read and write and do numbers. That's all. She's not gonna put a harness on you, or trim your toenails, for land's sakes."

Lester froze on the spot. "What are you talking about?"

"Good-bye, Lester. See you there, or won't see you there. I don't care." I walked off, following the slightly beaten path that led between our houses. Momma had made me bring the two old magazines, but I was embarrassed that Mrs. Berryman would think they were stupid. It was all I could read, and Momma thought it was important that I start off on the right foot, knowing something, or at least appearing that I did. But I was hoping Mrs. Berryman would let me read some of her real books, with their hard covers and golden edges.

As we approached the soddy, we could see two wagons sitting there. One was the shiny black one, and the other looked like the Whitfields'. It was. I could see Paulie sitting in the seat, tossing bits of something at the horse's rump, tormenting it as usual.

Seeing the two wagons, Lester grew twice as nervous. He held my hand and pressed his face into the back of my arm as we walked along. Paulie was singing, "Down, down, down, Downings in the well. Oh, hello, Downings." He was as nasty as a mean-tempered rooster, just looking for trouble.

I ignored him and met Mrs. Berryman coming out the

door of her soddy with her husband and the Whitfields.

"Now, remember," Doc was saying, "I won't be more than three or four days, and you'll be perfectly safe if you'll just do everything I told you." Mrs. Berryman seemed to be hanging on Doc's arm just like Lester was hanging on mine.

"I have left the gun with you, and some ammunition. There is plenty of water in the barrel—"

"Children!" Mrs. Berryman exclaimed when she saw us. "Oh, my students, I'm so glad you're here!" She put her arm around my shoulders and hugged me to her. I was shocked to feel her hands trembling so, and my head was rocked with the pounding of her heart as she drew me to her.

Doc Berryman climbed up on his wagon, and Mr. Whitfield got up beside him. "I think we're ready," Doc said, taking the reins into his hands.

"William, wait! Wait!" Mrs. Berryman ran around to his side of the wagon and pulled him down to her by the front of his jacket. She pressed her lips to his, long and hard, with all of us standing right there looking on. Her hand went up behind his head, and he struggled from her embrace, red-faced and fierce.

"Emmeline! Remember yourself, please!" He ran his fingers through his hair, tipping his hat and pushing it back in place. "Take care of things, dear," he said, and she backed off, hugging her arms to herself.

"Hurry back, William. Please." Her eyes filled with tears, and her fingers quickly wiped them away before they overflowed onto her cheeks. He drove off, never looking back, although Mr. Whitfield turned and waved his hat once in the air.

Never had the prairie seemed so empty to me as it did at that moment. I hadn't realized that a grown person could look so lonely and frightened. Lester whispered to me, "He shouldn't go away like that."

I shushed him.

Mrs. Berryman turned to us, and I noticed for the first time that one eyelid was fluttering uncontrollably. Paulie burped.

"Mrs. Berryman?" I said.

She stared at me as if she had just noticed I was there. "Louisa. Yes. Our lessons." She began to walk slowly to the door of the soddy. "Let's begin."

"Lessons?" Mrs. Whitfield was standing just outside the door, her arms folded over her bulk, and the front of her apron stained and stiff. "You're giving lessons, Emmeline?"

She turned and spoke weakly. "Yes, I am. Clara and I talked. I'll teach the children."

"Then, of course, you'll teach Paulie, too. Some numbers, so he can learn to help his father with the affairs, and writing and reading. . . ."

But Momma was doing Mrs. Berryman's laundry for

her. What would Mrs. Whitfield do except wait for Emmeline to give up and move back East? And besides, the thought of being with Paulie was sickening. How would I learn with him there?

"Well . . ." She hesitated and looked out at the disappearing form of her husband's wagon. "Of course. Come along, Paulie. You might as well join us." She disappeared into the darkness of her soddy, and Mrs. Whitfield jerked her head at Paulie.

"Go on, Paulie," she said. "Go learn something for a change."

"Like hell I—"

Lester and I ducked into the soddy, not missing the commotion of a few slaps and a howl from Paulie. He followed shortly after. The three of us kids stood there, watching Mrs. Berryman, who was in the middle of the room staring into space, wide-eyed, as if she were in a trance. She shook her head and pressed the palm of her hand to her forehead.

"Yes, yes," she murmured. "Have a seat here," she began, pulling the two chairs away from the table. She smoothed the cloth, but there was no cloth, just the dark wooden boards.

Lester and I sat down, leaving Paulie to stand fuming in the doorway. I watched as Mrs. Berryman went to her store of books. "Let's see," she said. "What shall we begin with?"

She turned and looked at us. Her shoulders sagged, and she seemed to be breathing deeply. "Oh, I'm glad you're here," she said. "I'm so very glad not to be alone right now.

"Lester," she added, "let Paulie sit there, sweetheart, because he and Louisa will have to do the hardest work. Come. Come here, and we'll pick out something you might like to hear." She knelt in front of her shelves of books and ran her finger over their bindings. She pulled one out, then another and another.

Lester had given up his seat, but he hesitated to go to her, hiding instead behind the little covering the chair offered. Paulie collapsed into the chair and glared at me. I tucked my feet under my seat.

When Mrs. Berryman came to the table, she was carrying three books. "Louisa, I'll start you on this. I brought it along thinking my own child might use it someday." She placed a dark-blue book before me. The cover said *Green's Universal Primer.* "And Paulie, how does this sound? One of Doc's books—*The Life of Jesse James?*"

Paulie bolted out of the soddy like a wildcat. He knocked over the chair and pushed the table board into my stomach. "Paulie!" Mrs. Berryman called after him. "Wait! Wait! Come back!"

Lester and I exchanged a glance. "He's a real hard character, Mrs. Berryman. I'm really glad to see him go."

She went to the door, and I could see his back running

off in the opposite direction of his house. "Yoo-hoo! Paulie!"
She shaded her eyes with her arm and waited. Then she
stared down at the book in her hand. "Maybe he doesn't
like Jesse James."

"Ha!" I laughed. "He thinks he *is* Jesse James."

"Well, I'll keep this right here for him, and I hope he'll
come back."

"I don't," I said softly, thumbing through the pages of
my book.

"Come, Lester, have a seat, then, and I'll get you started
with some letters." She opened the back of another book.
"I don't have much paper, so I want you to practice the
letters on the insides of the cover here, and you ask your
father if he can get you a slate the next time he goes to
town, all right? Until I can get more paper."

Lester slid onto the seat and circled his arms around
the book that lay on the table. She leaned over him with
a pencil in her hand and across the top of the page she
wrote: *A A A A A* and *a a a a a*, and then turned it back
to him.

"That's A, Lester. And it represents the sound 'a,' so
whenever you are reading and you see that letter, you
make the sound 'a.' Copy it now. All across, very neatly
and carefully, thinking about 'a.' "

Lester took the pencil in his hand and looked at it
carefully. He wound his fingers around it and applied it
warily to the inside cover of the book.

"Now, Louisa, let's see how well you can read, and then I will know what books you might be ready for."

I read then from her little blue book slowly and carefully, surprising even myself at what I was able to do, after what seemed like years of reading just two worn magazines and the labels on food packs and tins.

Lester got to the letter G that morning, and I read half the book real well, but I was disappointed that there was no special adventure in the reading. It was only like some preaching I had heard, and I knew there was more to it than that.

"We may chance, some time or other, to be left friendless in a strange country, and we shall then feel ever so glad if any kind people take notice of us, and give us food, or money to buy food with. We should always give to those who are in need, and if we do so, we shall be sure to get help when we ourselves are in need."

My voice droned on and on as Mrs. Berryman listened to me with great concentration, correcting me now and again and nodding her approval. Sometimes I would look up at her and lose my place. I was so pleased with myself.

Later, she pulled a book off her shelf, and closing my book and Lester's, she settled herself down on her bed and tucked her feet up under her. "Let me read to you awhile," she said.

She sat with the thick book on her lap and leafed through

the pages, wetting a finger softly on her tongue. "Let's see. Let's see. How about Tennyson?"

I shrugged. I was willing. I folded my arms on the table and rested my head on them. With one eye I could see her through the fine hairs of my arm. The wood on the table smelled good and echoed the quietness of my breath. She began.

> "With blackest moss the flower pots
> Were thickly crusted one and all;
> The rusted nails fell from the knots
> That held the pear to the gable wall."

She looked at me, her eyebrows arching on her pale face, her voice like Poppa's when he's telling a ghost story.

> "The broken sheds looked sad and strange:
> Unlifted was the clinking latch;
> Weeded and worn the ancient thatch
> Upon the lonely moated grange."

Lester slipped under the bed.

> "She only said, 'My life is dreary,
> He cometh not,' she said; . . ."

Mrs. Berryman's voice became quieter, her eyes went closer to the page, and, as if forgetting we were there, she whispered to herself,

"She said, 'I am aweary, aweary.
I would that I were dead!' "

Then her fingers were flying over the pages again. "No, no, let's see what else we can find. . . . How about this? It's called 'The Eagle; A Fragment.' You've seen eagles and hawks out here. What do you think of this?

"He clasps the crag with crooked hands;
Close to the sun in lonely lands,
Ring'd with the azure world, he stands.
The wrinkled sea beneath him crawls;
He watches from his mountain walls,
And like a thunderbolt he falls. . . ."

I went to her side then, anxious to see how that looked on the page, almost expecting to see a delicately etched drawing of a Nebraska hawk. Her finger was on words that were arranged in a shape like a box. A poem.

"Do you like that, Louisa?"

"Yes. Read it again." I looked at her. "Who wrote that? A congressman?"

She smiled. Her eyes were green, with light specks of brown that I had never noticed before. "Tennyson," she said, tucking a loose strand of hair behind my ear. "A poet, an English poet. He's not an American."

"You mean he's never been to Nebraska?"

She looked at the poem, puzzled. "Does that sound like Nebraska to you?"

My finger touched the second line. I read, "Close to the sun in lonely lands."

"Is Nebraska a lonely land to you, Louisa?" Her eyes searched mine.

I nodded.

"But I didn't think it would feel lonely after a while, or if you were born here. I didn't think you'd feel lonely anymore."

"I do"—how could I explain it?—"but it's nice."

She closed the book. "Aha! So that's the difference! You *like* being lonely."

She stood up and walked to the window, the deep window where she had stood that first day. Now it was not a surprise to her. We both knew exactly what was out the window. The lonely prairie, only to her it wasn't a comfort like it was to me, like the comfort of a blank wall without too many things on it, or a stretch of clean, flawless sand down at the river.

"If only I could see a red brick building casting a cool shadow, a crossing with horses and carriages and angry drivers, and cobblestone, and shops with the wares displayed on the sidewalks, and people in finery, and huge ships docked with their masts reaching up into the sky." She spun around and looked at me expectantly. "You would love it, Louisa. It's exciting and lively and sociable,

and my family's there and my friends, and bookshops to browse in, and dressmakers' shops, and fish! I'll bet you've never eaten a fish."

"I have," I said, feeling a little put off.

"Well, maybe you have, but not crabs or lobsters or clams, and there are seashells on the beach."

"There are seashells out here in the riverbeds," I told her.

She collapsed on the bed, suddenly looking worn and tired. "You'll have to show me, then. You mean there's really more than grass?"

"Sure! There's shells, and arrowheads, and bull snakes, and lizards, and shooting stars and rainbows, and—"

She sat there staring at me, and her eyelid began to dance again as I watched. She smoothed her hand over her eye and said, "I think that's enough for today."

"Can we come back tomorrow?" Lester asked, his head peeking up over the edge of the straw mattress.

"I'm *counting* on you coming back tomorrow," she said, leaning forward and holding his chin in her hand. "You are such good students. Tell me," she said shyly, "am I a good teacher, do you think so?"

"Oh, yes!" Lester jumped up and looked at her solemnly.

"And do you think you'll read out loud for me someday, Lester?"

He shook his head and backed off from her easy touch.

"Oh, Lester, I know you can learn those letters so easily, and then you will say them for me, and put them together, and then you'll have words. You'll be reading. Right out loud, but in your own time, I know."

"To myself," he corrected. "Inside."

She stood and arched her back with her hands pressing on her hips. "You'll see, Lester. When you're ready." Her belly stuck way out and we could hear a tiny bone crack deep inside her. She smiled.

"Well, I'll see you children tomorrow morning. I won't rest again till you're back to keep me company." She walked with us to the door. I picked up Momma's old magazines and tucked them under my arm.

"Ma'am?"

"Yes, Louisa?"

"Do you think I could take one of your books home to read? To practice some?"

"I think it would be all right. Which would you like? Any one in particular?"

"How about Hannah's son?"

"Tennyson? You like that? Well, read it slowly, and just read one poem at a time, slowly and deliciously, like good pudding, yes?"

"Yes, ma'am." She put the thick book in my hand.

"The eagle poem is marked with the ribbon here," she said, pointing to the binding. "And Lester?"

He looked in the direction of our home out the door.

"You remember to ask your father if he can put together some sort of slate for you soon. For practicing your letters."

He ran off without me.

"Thank you, Mrs. Berryman. Momma says she'll be doing laundry day after tomorrow, so send some things home with me tomorrow."

"All right. I appreciate that."

I smiled at her and backed away from the soddy, realizing at that moment, as I think she did, that I was leaving her all alone. All alone for the first time since Doc Berryman left. She just stood in the doorway of the soddy and watched us walk away. Each time I turned back, she was still there, like a stone statue.

I knew Momma was alone. But Momma wasn't scared about it. I'll bet she even favored it a bit, as I did, to be so free and alone, like that hawk spreading his wings and flying, with yourself being the only noise you could hear and the only sight you could see.

Once the soddy disappeared behind the rise, I kept looking back now and then, half expecting Mrs. Berryman to come running after us.

Chapter Seven

There's nothing worse than washday, jerking that stick back and forth in each tub of laundry for eternities, with my arms aching. But it was a little better with Mrs. Berryman come visiting, and Momma saying more than "Keep washing, Louisa. There's more to do."

The two women were admiring our two trees, two sticks

nearly as tall as me, with tiny fringes of precious three-sided leaves.

"Cottonwood," Momma said. "I brought them up from the Loup and planted them three years ago. J.T. promised me they wouldn't take up here. 'You'll have to water them like I water the cattle, Clara,' he told me." She smiled and rubbed a leaf between her fingers. "But it's worth it. One day they'll shade the house and make for a nice place to sit on a summer night. They took. They took fine."

Mrs. Berryman was quiet, like she didn't appreciate how special those two sticks were and how Momma coddled them sometimes as if they were babies.

"There's a linden at home," she said. "It's tremendous, tall and wide, and the branches just swoop down and touch the ground all around. It's wonderful." Mrs. Berryman cupped a plain cottonwood leaf in her palm. "I can't say I ever remember anyone watering it, though."

"That's too bad," Momma said. "I think everyone should have something in their life that they need to carry water to. Heavy water." She smiled. "And far."

Mrs. Berryman turned to scan the horizon. "Maybe so," she said quietly.

Later we all spread the freshly laundered clothes out to dry on the grass, and hung the small things on the knot of antelope horns at the corner of the soddy. Momma began emptying the tubs of water, one bucketful at a time, at the base of her two trees.

"Let me help," Mrs. Berryman offered, reaching for the bucket. "I can do that."

The weight of the water forced her to lean away from it, and she looked like a lumbering bear, her feet wide apart in her steps, her huge belly thrust way out before her, and her free arm waving about. She poured out the water, and then stood with her hand pressed to the small of her back, the other hand shading her eyes. Once again she looked off in the direction of the path on which Momma had said Doc might return.

"Clara?"

Momma was coming with another bucket. The water gushed onto the skinny tree trunk and was immediately soaked up by the dry baked earth.

"I do believe that's a wagon."

Momma looked, too. "Yes, you're right."

Mrs. Berryman took off her hat and smoothed her hair. "Oh, my, I feel like a schoolgirl waiting for her beau." She smoothed her skirts, twisted the cuffs on her blouse and the collar of her dress. Patting her belly, she laughed. "But I hardly look like a schoolgirl, do I?"

Momma and Mrs. Berryman went back to the shade of the soddy and watched the wagon approach. All around them were sheets and socks and blouses and billowing skirts and aprons and trousers. They would be dry in little time, the sun being so hot. A slight breeze would come up now and then and make a skirt dance gently or take a cotton sock skipping across the prairie.

Lester and I ran to meet the wagon, keeping an eye on the dust that was rising up behind it. Closer and closer. Doc Berryman waved, and when it grew near enough for us to hear the wheels turning, Lester turned and ran back to the house. I went on alone, and Mr. Whitfield slowed the wagon and hoisted me up beside him.

"Well, hello there, little Louise," the doc said, always mispronouncing my name. "Have you been taking good care of Mrs. Berryman for me?"

"Yes, sir, I mean, no, sir. She's been taking care of herself pretty much. Today's the first day she's been over. It's washday."

He squeezed my nose between his two fingers and laughed. "Washday, huh?"

"Anybody sick?" I asked.

He looked at me curiously. "Why, Louise, you aiming to be a nurse or something? Want to go doctoring with me?"

"No, sir. Just wondering."

He didn't answer my question but gazed ahead at the sight of Momma and Mrs. Berryman standing waiting. Momma seemed brown and tan, like a small squirrel holding very still, and Mrs. Berryman, next to her, all pinks and blues, was clapping her hands and waving.

"William! William!" she called.

Mr. Whitfield chuckled. "Looks like you've been missed, Doc. My missus will have a list of chores and complaints waiting for me. 'Carney, do this. Carney, do that.' Look at that pretty blossom waiting for you."

Doc seemed to flush, and he rubbed the back of his neck roughly. "More like a hothouse flower, if you need to know the truth."

Hothouse flower. I had visions of a flower blooming in a house that would catch fire. Hothouse flower.

She was at the side of the wagon, and before she could pull him out of his seat, he jumped down and turned her around playfully.

"Good Lord, Emmeline! You have gained another hundred pounds! Whew!"

"Oh, it's not me, William. It's this little son of yours, growing and growing."

She clung to him and kissed his ear. He held her away from him. "I have a little bit of disappointing news for you, Emmeline. Well, first the good news, and then the bad. How about that?"

Her fingers tapped nervously on her belly. "What? All right. First the good news."

He lifted a covered package from the seat as Mr. Whitfield got down to tend to the horse.

"Can I offer you some cold tea, Carney? Doc?" Momma asked.

"Yes, Mrs. Downing. That would be lovely." The doc held out the present for his wife. "For you, darling. To keep you company." He slipped the cover off. It was a small metal cage painted white, and inside was a plump yellow bird that was frantically jumping from perch to perch.

"Oh, how lovely. How precious!" Mrs. Berryman said, holding the cage up close to her face, and the bird chirped thin musical notes that startled us all. "Lester! Louisa! Look!" We had never seen a real canary before, not alive anyway. Once this family came by, going east, leaving Nebraska, and they stayed with us. The woman kept her canary in a small box, dead, nestled in lacy Valentine paper. Alive was better. I couldn't take my eyes off that bird. It was so different from the birds I knew. More like a piece of candy or a Christmas decoration than a bird.

It quieted down on one perch and sang.

"Oh, William, wherever did you find this?"

"At the depot. A few had come in, and the stationmaster gave it to me as kind of an apology."

"An apology?"

Momma was tapping my head. "Louisa, come help me with the drinks," she said, starting off toward the soddy.

"Wait, Momma," I said. "I just want to hear the bad news."

"Louisa, now!"

I saw Mrs. Berryman look up at her husband's face with a question in her eyes. An apology? The bad news?

I ran backward after Momma, watching the doc walk Mrs. Berryman around to the back of the wagon. I stood in the doorway, not daring to take my eyes off them for a minute, not wanting to miss the bad news.

"Louisa!" Momma scolded. "Mind your own business."

"But, Momma—"

"Fetch the glasses, right now."

I reached to the shelf for glasses just as the scream pierced the air. Momma and I looked at each other, and I turned and ran from the soddy before she could say a word.

Mrs. Berryman was standing with her hands over her mouth. The cage was at her feet, turned on its side, and the doc was pulling pieces of wood from the back of the wagon, picking them up and putting them down again. "That's how it arrived," he said.

"Oh, no, oh, no," she was saying over and over again. Next to her, I could see into the wagon at the carton that was busted up and crushed, rough splintery wood like the bark of a tree, and mixed with them were dark-red pieces of polished wood with twists and curlicues and carvings. They were splintered, too.

Mrs. Berryman's trembling hands were tearing at the box, pulling at the dark pieces and clutching them in her arms. "You must fix it, William, you must." Her face was wild, splotched and flushed, and her eye was twitching madly again. "Fix it!" she screamed at the doctor. "Fix it!"

"Emmeline, please. Control yourself. It's silly to feel so

upset. It's hopelessly splintered and broken. It's no use. I'm sorry, and the man at the depot felt—"

"The man at the depot!" she shrieked, her eyes burning into him, the splintered wood spilling out of her arms. "This is for your son! So your son doesn't come into this world to live like a savage, stuffed in a drawer!"

I held my breath. Did she think *I* was a savage? Poppa had called me "little sparrow" when I was little enough to sleep in a drawer. Mrs. Berryman seemed hard and brittle to me for the first time, like her broken crate. Doc eyed me nervously, and out of the corner of my eye, I caught the shadow of Momma disappearing into the soddy. I knew she had heard it, too.

"Emmeline, please—"

"Don't Emmeline me." She dropped the wood on the ground and stood there panting. Her fingers stood out rigidly like spokes of a wagon wheel. I could see her eye. "This is a sign, William," she whispered hoarsely. "A sign."

"You are being absurd—"

"See your broken crib?"

"Emmeline, now—"

"See your broken crib?"

He said nothing.

"It's a sign, Doctor Berryman." She spoke through clenched teeth. "As the cradle is destroyed, so are you destroying me and your own child."

Mr. Whitfield suddenly had me by the arm and was steering me into the house.

Momma was standing in the shadows, horror-stricken. "Dear God," she whispered.

Mr. Whitfield rubbed his beard and glanced out the door. "Maybe this was a mistake, Clara. This is not going to work. Pru was right. The doc's all right, but that woman is going to put it all awry."

"It's the child," Momma said. "That's all. Women do the craziest things, say crazy things, when they're carrying a child. It's the heaviness, the awkwardness speaking."

"I think not," Mr. Whitfield said. "I think it's the refinement and the city speaking. There's no place for that out here. Fancy cribs! Tons of books. Jeez, Pru is going to have my hide."

Doc Berryman was at the door.

"Carney, I'm leaving. I have to go back. With the wagon." He was shaken. "Can you get home all right? I need to get Emmeline home and into bed. Her nerves."

Mr. Whitfield waved him on. "Go ahead, Doc. Take care of your family. I'll get back fine."

We watched out the door as Doc Berryman climbed into his wagon and took off. Mrs. Berryman wasn't with him. She was walking some distance ahead toward her soddy, the cage under one arm and a bundle of broken dark wood under the other.

He rode alongside her, and we could tell he was speaking

to her, but she walked on, heavily, straight ahead, not looking up at him.

"Emmeline, Emmeline, please," reached us on the breeze, and we watched as one of Emmeline's long white stockings drying on the grass suddenly lifted up and trotted away from us all.

Chapter Eight

Our lessons continued at the Berrymans' soddy as if nothing had happened. Some days Doc was there while we read. Once he even read to us himself, his smooth voice rhyming out the words. He could even look away from the page sometimes and still know the words, as if he had memorized much of it. There was one long poem that he read, and all I remember now was the image of a red sun glaring through the ribs of a phantom ship. I can remember the fine hairs on my arms standing up as he spoke.

Some days we got to see his patients: a man from the railroad, stopping to have a broken arm checked; and a family came from twenty miles off with their little child. The mother held him in her lap while the doc sewed his eyebrow back on his forehead. He screamed, that little child, and the blood was all over his mother's dress once the doctor started. Seems I would have rather had a hanging eyebrow the rest of my life than to go through that.

Mrs. Berryman made us do our lessons out in the narrow shade of the soddy that day, but we could still hear the screaming and Doc's soft, gentle voice. Mrs. Berryman sat down on the ground with us, nervous and twittering like her trapped bird. Lester and me pretended we were busy reading, but we watched as she pressed her fingers secretly into her ears. Between the screaming and Mrs. Berryman, we had a lot to tell Momma when we got home.

"Emmeline sounds like she's getting worse," Poppa had said to Momma. "She's getting a wild kind of look in her eye."

"And this one lid," I added, "keeps twitching and jerking around like—"

"Louisa! Enough!" Momma dried her wet hands on the towel and glared at me. "Leave the poor woman alone. She's doing the best she can, and I'm sure once the baby is born, she'll be more herself. This is a trying time for her."

Poppa wet his hands and ran them through his hair. "Maybe you're right, Clara. Maybe so." He smiled sheepishly at her. "Remember when you were carrying Lester and you attacked the vegetable garden with an ax?"

Momma glared at him, and then at me. I had never heard this one before.

"Only after the locusts had totally destroyed it, J.T. And you know it. Weeks of lugging water from the river, the tomatoes just beginning to blush on the vine . . ." She stared off into space. "This is a country that can drive you mad, that's for certain."

"You attacked the garden with an ax, Momma?"

She pursed her lips and pushed the red bucket at me impatiently. "Go get some berries for dinner. Take your brother with you."

Her look told me the subject was closed, and as I passed through the garden on the way to the berries, I tried to imagine my mother with an ax, swinging it at the tomato stakes, the pea strings, the cucumber trellis. "Drive you mad," she had said. Drive you mad.

Mrs. Berryman's tremblings and twitchings were strange to me, filling me more with curiosity than horror. But after the day Paulie got ahold of the gun, well, she began to crumble slowly and surely like an abandoned soddy in the hot prairie sun. And I just wasn't sure I wanted to go back to that soddy anymore, books or no books.

We were arriving for our lessons, and the day was feeling cooler and breezy. Paulie had never come back to our lessons, but when Mrs. Berryman's soddy was in sight we realized the Whitfields' wagon was there again, and Mrs. Whitfield and Mrs. Berryman were out in front talking.

"You just need to be strong with him, Emmeline," Mrs. Whitfield was saying. "Don't let him get away with anything, you hear? He needs a mean hand to keep him in place, and you just rap him with your ruler. Isn't that what you teachers do?"

"I don't think I could hit him, Pru, and please, if he doesn't want to come, don't force him. I really don't feel up to teaching anyone who needs to be forced." She turned and peered into the soddy, where I guessed Paulie was. "Maybe he'd just like to take one of the books with him, and kind of study on his own." She hooked her fingers nervously in the collar of her dress. "I really don't think . . ."

I saw the look of rage on Mrs. Whitfield's face before I realized what was happening. In the doorway of the Berrymans' soddy stood Paulie Whitfield, with a mean smirk on his face. I swear I thought of Jesse James. His legs were spread wide and straight, and on his shoulder, aimed true at his mother, was the Berrymans' rifle. The one they kept over the door. The one Mrs. Berryman would use to frighten away coyotes and Indians.

He walked slowly up to his mother, one eye closed and the other focused down the barrel of the rifle, slowly, slowly, his bare feet sure and steady in the grass.

"Get in the wagon, Ma," he ordered.

"Paulie, you put that down." She was backing up, her arms held away from her sides.

"Into the wagon, Ma," he repeated.

"Paulie, your pa is gonna—"

A blast exploded at her feet, and the hem of her skirt tore from her and flapped on the ground. Lester had his arms around my waist and was trembling something fierce.

"Into the wagon, Ma."

Mrs. Whitfield held her hands in the air and backed up to the standing wagon. She slammed into it hard, and then turned, never taking her eyes off her son as she climbed up into the seat.

I stepped back slowly, as in a dream where nothing moves fast enough. I tried to get to the soddy, to hide around the back, to take Lester with me. Was that Lester screaming?

I rubbed my hands on his arms roughly, to shush him. I thought Paulie would turn and shoot us, when I suddenly realized it wasn't Lester screaming, but Mrs. Berryman. Like blasts from a train whistle, she screamed and screamed and screamed, her fingers rigid in her hair, her eyes seeming to bulge out of her face.

Lester's arms were around me like a bull snake. Paulie

had eyes only for his mother. He had jammed the end of the rifle into her behind as she scrambled up into the seat. He laughed.

And then, before I knew what had happened, Doc Berryman was behind Paulie. Although Paulie was my age, he was much taller, almost as tall as the doc. But Doc slipped his arm around Paulie's neck from behind and pulled him backward.

Paulie gagged, and Mrs. Whitfield held her hands up to her stricken face. "Paulie!" she cried.

Doc jerked him and said, "Drop it."

Nothing happened, and he jerked Paulie by the neck again. "I said, drop it."

Nothing.

Mrs. Berryman had stopped screaming, but her breathing seemed loud and unnatural. I looked at her to see her skirt pulled up over her face and her head. Her whole body was twitching and shaking. I think that's when I started to cry.

I looked back at Doc in time to see Paulie drop the rifle—butt, then barrel—to the ground at his feet. And then Doc picked him up by his neck and the seat of his pants and threw him onto the hard floor of the wagon. Mrs. Whitfield sobbed. The loud clunk must have been Paulie's head. He didn't reappear, but I could still hear him gagging.

"Get him out of here!" shouted Doc. I had never seen

anyone so angry. His neck bulged out of the top of his tight collar, and he picked up his rifle and aimed it at the wagon. "Get him out of here, and if I ever see him within a mile of my home, I'll kill him like I would a mangy coyote."

Mrs. Whitfield slapped the reins on her horse and cried loudly as she drove away. She was yelling something, but I couldn't tell if she was yelling at Paulie or the doc or her horse.

Lester released me and ran panic-stricken toward home. He stumbled and fell, and got up and kept running. I stood, undecided about running after him or just taking root right where I was, paralyzed with my own fear. But Doc made up my mind for me.

"Louise! Get me some water!"

Mrs. Berryman was lying on the ground, with her skirt still up over her head, and her stomach thrust into the air like a mound of earth.

"Louise! Now!"

He knelt beside her and murmured to her, smoothing down her skirt, fanning her face, and patting her hands. When I came out of the house, he had his ear pressed to the bulge of the baby and was very still. He laid his hands to her taut belly. When I handed him the glass of water, he tossed it right in her face.

She didn't move. Her cheeks were limp and colorless. He reached out and pushed me away, and then he wedged his arms beneath her. As he lifted her, her head fell backward and her skirts dragged in the dirt. "Emm, Emm," he was saying.

As he stepped into the soddy, water suddenly gushed from beneath her skirt as if a bucket had been kicked over. I backed up, and he disappeared inside, trailing water, calling her, and forgetting I was there.

I think I cried all the way home. Sobbing and moaning. Something was terribly wrong. I just knew it. When I got back to the soddy, exhausted and out of breath, Momma was waiting, with Lester hidden behind her skirts.

"Louisa! I was just going to go get you. Are you all right?" Her arms went around me, and I let myself go with the crying, like I hadn't cried since I was a baby.

"Paulie didn't hurt anyone, did he? And Doc got him to leave?"

Lester was there, patting my arm, looking into my face.

"Paulie's gone." I sobbed. "But something awful is happening."

"What?" Momma's face was level with mine, her hands on my shoulders. She shook me. "What, child?"

"Mrs. Berryman. She's dead."

"Dead?"

"She fell down, and all water poured out of her."

Momma straightened. "That's not dead, Louisa. That's the baby coming." She wrung her hands, took a step toward the barn and then back to look at me again.

"Louisa?"

"What?"

"I'm going to go to Doc's to help him. The baby is coming too early. He might need some help."

She hugged Lester to her. "I want you to take care of things here. Poppa's out in the southern cornfields and should be back at dinner. You hear? Louisa?" she shouted.

"Yes, yes."

"Take care of Lester. Do the chores. I might be a long time."

Lester clung to her and began to cry. Momma peeled him off and pushed him toward me. "Lester, stay with your sister till Poppa gets back. You'll be fine. Doc might need help."

"Is she dead? Is she dead?" Lester said, sobbing.

"No, Lester. She's not dead. Now get inside. Or go get some vegetables for dinner, or eggs." Momma began running to the barn, yelling out directions, and Lester and I stood there watching her, our arms around each other, scared, ignorant about what was happening, and wanting Poppa to hurry back, and Momma. And for all this trouble to be over.

Chapter Nine

When Momma wasn't home by dinner, Poppa told me to fill up a basket with food. "We'll ride over and see how things are," he said. He ran his fingers through his black hair and walked aimlessly around the soddy. "Maybe I should bring something. I wonder what they need."

Lester went under the bed. "I don't wanna go."

"Lester, get out of there." Poppa's voice was impatient, but Lester didn't come out. "I have no time for your nonsense. You are coming with me, and that's all."

I was scared, too, but careful not to show it. Poppa turned to me. His voice was angry. "I'm going to get the wagon ready. You get him outside." And he left.

I packed the bread and wrapped some eggs carefully and poured out a big jar of soup. I even put in the can of pineapple that we were saving for next Christmas. Momma would understand, and maybe it would help Mrs. Berryman cheer up a little.

"Come on out, Lester. You heard Poppa."

"I'm scared."

"Well, that's silly. What's to be scared of?"

"Paulie, and Doc Berryman, and Mrs. B-b-berryman screaming, and . . . and—" Lester began to sob.

"Lester, stop it, you hear?" I reached under the bed and pulled out his ankle. I held his leg in my lap, not sure what to do with it. I rubbed it slowly at first. "Poppa will be with us. You shouldn't be afraid."

"I am." He sobbed. "I'm scared."

I squeezed his ankle hard. "That's stupid. Now git out here before I get in trouble. You hear? You're afraid of everything that's not nailed down, and I'm sick of it." I pulled him harder, knocking over the empty slop jar, but he must have had a grip on the other side of the bed. "This is no fooling around, now git out!"

"No, Louisa, no," he pleaded.

I crawled under the bed with him and met him face to face. "Poppa's going. And I'm going with him to see Momma." I made my voice scary. "And if you don't come, you'll be here all alone. All alone, and maybe Paulie will come after you, or Indians."

He started to bawl louder, if that was possible.

"Now git out in that wagon and shut up if you know what's good for you, 'cause I think Poppa would just as soon drive off and leave you right here."

Lester grabbed my skirt in his small trembling fist. "Don't leave me, please. Stay here with me."

I pried his hands open and began to ease myself away. "All alone, Lester, and who knows, maybe some hungry coyotes will be passing by, and—mmmmm—smell some nice boy in that there soddy, howling his brains out."

Lester was coming after me. "Don't leave me."

A shadow fell across the floor, and Poppa was standing in the doorway. "Your Momma took the wagon?"

"Yes, Poppa."

He frowned at us, sitting there on the floor. "We best walk then." He held out his hand. "Come on. Let's move it before it gets dark."

Lester's arms were curled around himself, but he walked slowly to Poppa, who looked down on him kind of hard, I thought. "Stand up, boy. I have no use for a scaredy-cat girl the likes of you."

Lester sobbed.

"I said, stand up."

Lester's arms dropped to his sides, and he lifted his chin to look at Poppa. "Yes, Poppa."

Poppa glared at him and held out his hand. "Come on, now." And then they left me alone in the soddy to gather up the rest of the things and run after them. By the time I reached them, Lester was sitting on Poppa's shoulders, his head propped on Poppa's head. And it was a good thing Poppa couldn't see him, because big quiet tears were running down his cheeks and into Poppa's hair.

I hooked my finger in Poppa's belt loop, and we walked along to the Berrymans' soddy. There is nothing in this world like walking a few miles on a prairie, the ground just passing under your feet, the dust, the grass, just more and more of nothing in the bowl of the never-changing earth. Lester was sniffling, and Poppa took long, slow, steady steps, one step for every three of mine. The basket kept smacking against my leg, and the sounds of our steps, the quiet lapping of the soup in the jar, Lester's delicate snorts, all made a kind of music I still remember today. It was a sad song. I can remember so clearly that walk to the Berrymans' soddy, clear as the table before me, but I cannot remember at all the walk back home, and yet I know we must've walked, because we left the wagon for Momma.

There was no sign of life from the Berrymans' soddy.

Not a soul was in sight but poor Cap, who was standing off a distance, still hitched to the wagon.

For a minute I thought a hawk was screeching, or a horse was being torn or murdered. I stopped short in my tracks, tightening the grip on my father's belt loop. He stopped, too, and looked down at me uncertainly, as if deciding something. Lester's legs began to tremble down each side of Poppa's chest. "Get down, boy," he said, lifting Lester off and setting him on the ground. "Sounds like Mrs. Berryman is still having that baby."

He scratched his head. He thought. He didn't move. "Why don't you two wait here? I'll be back in a minute."

"No!" Lester shouted, clinging to his leg.

The scream died away.

Poppa walked quickly to the soddy without saying another word, and we ran behind him. At the door he hesitated and then called quietly, "Clara?"

Something banged inside, and Momma was at the door, pale and shaken. She closed the door behind her and stepped out to us.

"J.T., children. I was thinking about you, hoping you were getting along all right."

"And you? How are you?" Poppa touched her arm and looked back at the soddy.

Momma walked away from us, as if to lure us away from something unpleasant. She slipped an arm around each of our shoulders. "Poor Emmeline is having a rough time.

It's taking long, and it's hard, but soon she'll have a nice baby, and all this will be forgotten."

I didn't believe her. Something in her voice told me it was what she wanted to believe herself, but didn't.

"We brought some dinner for you and the Berrymans, Momma. And I took along the can of pineapple from Aunt Winona."

"That's fine, Louisa." She wasn't listening to me. "Lester, are you feeling all right? You look weary."

"Just giving way to his girlish fears, Clara," Poppa said. "Don't baby him now."

But Momma picked Lester up in her arms and smiled at Poppa. "Hush, now. Lester has had a frightful day, nothing girlish about that." He looked foolish in her arms, his long legs dangling down her skirts, but he held fast until a bone-crunching scream came out of the soddy.

It was followed by a cry of "William! Will! Will!" Momma buried her face in Lester's neck.

"I should go," she said. She set Lester down and reached out to kiss Poppa. "Doc is doing all he can, and she is a workhorse, a pillar of strength, despite what everyone thinks of her." Momma kissed me, and kissed me again. I held out the basket to her, and she took it and turned back to the soddy. As she opened the door we heard Doc's voice, tight and strained, telling her something. Poppa just stared after her and then down at us.

"Let's feed Cap and put him away for the night. Momma can hitch him up again later when she's ready to come home." We followed Poppa to the stable and waited while he fed Cap, but we cringed in terror each time a scream filled the air.

I thought of the hothouse flower, a bright rainbow flower in a jar, set on a wooden table. And as it burst into flames, that's exactly how it would sound, the hard, grunting scream of Mrs. Berryman. I wouldn't have children, ever. I pressed my fists into my stomach. It would never grow. I wouldn't let it grow and grow until I burst into flames.

Momma never came home that night, or the next day. Poppa put us to bed that second night, tucking us in different than Momma did. He pressed the blanket tight around my body, till I was like a long snake stretched out on my bed. He pressed his warm lips to my cheek and tucked my hair behind my ears, tucking, tucking. And then he did Lester, but when he kissed Lester, Lester hugged him tight and then quickly let go. "Momma coming home tonight?"

"I hope so, son. It's a full moon, and it's still bright. She may try to come home tonight if it's over."

The soddy was softly lit by the one kerosene lamp on the wooden table. I closed my eyes, and I could still see the faint glow even behind my eyelids. There was not a sound except Poppa's footsteps as he walked to the deep window well and looked out. I couldn't tell if he was looking at the sky, or for Momma, or just at his own reflection in the small glass windows.

The sound of Cap's hooves woke me. I didn't realize I had fallen asleep, but now Poppa was getting up from the table. He went to the door and opened it, and Momma walked in, limp and quiet. She hadn't even put Cap away, or the wagon. She just came in and stood stone still in the middle of the room. It was very late, and I wasn't sure if Lester was asleep or not. I stayed quiet, horrified at the sound of my mother's uneven breathing. It seemed she was trying to take long breaths, but they turned into trembling sobs.

"The baby died, J.T. Died in my arms."

I could see Poppa put his arms around her and pull her to him. "It's over now, Clara," he murmured. "It's done."

Momma's sobs filled the room, and Poppa patted her and shushed her like a child. "How is Emmeline?" he asked. "Is she all right now?"

"She's alive. Barely. Half alive, knowing her baby's dead. Doc couldn't do anything. All that doctoring know-how, and there was just nothing he could do that I couldn't have done all by myself. It just went on and on." She collapsed into the chair, and I heard Lester move next to me. He was awake, too.

"And then when the baby came, a tiny boy, Doc took one look at the gray little child, and I guess he knew there was just no hope. He worked and worked on Emmeline.

She was bleeding so." Momma grew quiet. "Oh, J.T., I'm sorry to be going on like this."

Poppa pulled a chair alongside her. "It's over now, Clara."

"But I held that baby, J.T., and he wouldn't breathe. You have no idea. He just jerked a little, and I tried to keep him warm, give him life, but I couldn't. I couldn't do it." She began to cry.

"Shhhhh, now," Poppa said. "You did all you could."

"Momma?" Lester's whisper seemed to shatter the air in the room, as if he had given away the secret that we were listening. "Momma? The baby died?"

"Yes, sweetheart." She walked slowly to our beds and sat down near Lester. Her hair was down her back, and her face was all swollen. "The baby died. He was just too weak and little to live. Come," she said, drawing back the blankets. "Come let me feel how alive you are."

I sprang up, too, and both Lester and me went into her arms. She was trembling and began to rock us. I felt Poppa gather the blanket up around the three of us, and I closed my eyes. We rocked slowly in big rocking movements, back and forth, as vast as the Milky Way, as wide and as far as the prairie.

"Momma?" Lester asked.

"What, honey?"

"Am I gonna die, Momma?"

"Oh, no, Lester, no."

"Are you gonna die, Momma?"

"No, no, sweetie, not me."

"Just Delilah, Momma? That's all?"

"Just Delilah," she answered. "Just Delilah, that's all."

And then Momma began to cry, a sad mournful lament that I had never heard before and I have never heard since. I must have fallen asleep in Momma's arms that night.

Chapter Ten

The next day when Poppa went out to the Loup
to dig the grave, he told me to go with him. He
let me carry the shovel, and when we got there,
he stood back quietly and waited while I picked the spot.
I had picked Delilah's, too, and now I paced off ten steps
from Delilah's small grave and reminded him to point it
east. Poppa broke the ground, and I buttoned my sweater

up to my neck, staring out at the wide Loup rushing along. Winter was bearing down on us with the heaviness of a stubborn bull. I could feel it, and I shivered.

"It feels so cold out here," I said.

"The dead don't feel," he answered.

I tried not to watch the hole getting deeper, and instead I collected sprigs of dying wildflowers and leaves and stuck them in the ground around Delilah. Before, it had been a single grave. Now it would be a graveyard, a burial ground, blessed and holy, holding two. Why was it that just the babies were dying? I didn't know. But I knew I was glad that we weren't burying Mrs. Berryman, and that it was my baby sister I missed so much, and not my Momma.

"Here he comes," Poppa said, stopping and pointing off to the path. The sky was gray with a troubled light, and outlined against it was the brittle shape of a wagon. Doc Berryman was slumped in the seat, alone, and when the wagon turned to follow the path toward us, I saw the small trunk in the wagon bed behind him.

I stood by silently and watched the two men shake hands without speaking, and then Doc lifted the trunk and carried it to the grave Poppa had dug.

"Thank you, J.T.," Doc said, and he got down on his knees beside the grave, and he and Poppa lowered it down together, awkwardly, with simple directions to each other. Then they rose, and Doc brushed off his pants. Poppa just stood there. He wasn't a man of fancy words or prayers, but he was a thoughtful man. He stood there and thought.

It was too long, too long with no one speaking, until at last Poppa held the shovel out to Doc and stepped past him. I followed Poppa home. I slipped my hand in his when we came within sight of the soddy, trying to listen all the while to the sound of our footsteps and not to the slow scrape of the shovel growing fainter behind us.

Winter came, and no one mentioned starting up the lessons again. Lester was glad of it. Said he didn't care if he never learned to read. He knew enough as it was. All he had to do was learn to farm and build, and he wouldn't ever need reading, or any more of Mrs. Berryman—or Paulie, either, for that matter. I wasn't so sure. I missed the lessons. I was hoping that maybe, if the Berrymans didn't go back to New York, Mrs. Berryman would want us back someday soon and I'd get to read all her other books.

"You've got to learn," I told Lester. "Soon there will be more people out here, and real schools with desks and slates and books all over. And then you'll *have* to go to school, Lester, so you might as well start thinking about it, and getting ready. If you can't go to a simple school with just me and a teacher, what are you going to do when there are bigger schools and lots of people?"

"There are no 'lots of people' around here," he answered.

"Well, there will be, Momma says. Cities and towns and civilizations and stimulation."

Lester left me at that point. I was alone in the cellar,

churning the cream, waiting for the butter to come. "See that?" I called after him. "A few big words and you run scared. I swear, Lester, you'll be in big trouble when things start to catch on around here."

I heard a wagon outside then, and climbed the steps to peer out. It was Doc's wagon. Doc, and, sure enough, Mrs. Berryman was sitting right there next to him. I was surprised at how small she looked. I came up into the cold air, pulling my heavy jacket around me.

They didn't see me there and sat very still in the wagon, the wind whipping around them. I could hear Doc talking and pounding his hand against the wagon seat. "And you must . . ." The wind whipped away some words. ". . . if you think you can ever . . . there's only one thing to do, Emmeline. Now come down and stop this foolishness."

He climbed down and gave his hand to Mrs. Berryman. She stepped down, small, and straight up and down, the pleasant bulge of her belly gone.

"Hello," I said.

Her face turned toward me, and it was so like a skeleton's face that I caught my breath. There was just a thin veil of skin over her sharp cheekbones.

She answered me weakly. "Hello, Louisa."

"We've come to see your mother," Doc said. "Can you tell her we're here?"

"Sure." I started toward the door, but Momma was already there.

"Come in. Come in." Doc and Mrs. Berryman entered the soddy, and I scooted in after them. Momma surprised me by hugging Mrs. Berryman. A long, quiet hug.

"Emmeline," Momma said, holding her at arm's length. "You still look so tired. You must eat."

She nodded but didn't say a word.

"That's exactly what I've been telling her, Clara, but she's a stubborn woman." Doc took off his coat and tossed it onto my bed. He helped his wife out of her heavy shawl. Her elbows were like arrowheads pressed against her sleeves. I could see the tiny ringed bones down her neck. She coughed.

"Life is full of trials and tests, and we need to get on with life, and not give in so easily," he continued.

I saw Momma frown as she turned from him. "Let me put on some coffee," she said. "You must be cold. And I've made some cookies for the children. We can have some. And sit and talk. Are you warm enough in here? Come, sit by the stove."

Mrs. Berryman stood there next to the doctor and closed her eyes. Simply closed them as if she would never open them again. But Doc steered her toward the chair near the stove. "Emm," he said quietly, as if calling her back.

She sat down and looked at her hands. I had never seen her hands like that before, broken nailed and rough, one nail torn from her finger. Even lying in her iap, her fingers continued to move aimlessly.

"I think it's time to begin lessons again," the doctor announced. He looked at his wife expectantly.

"Yes," she said. "We'll have lessons again." Her voice was limp.

Momma turned from the stove and looked at each of them. "I don't know," she said softly. "I can't imagine this is a good time."

"Of course it is, Clara." The doctor cleared his throat. I had the peculiar feeling he had said these words over and over again. "We can't let life's trials conquer us. My own mother lost three children, but she just got back up on her feet and kept living."

Mrs. Berryman's head rolled back, and she stared up at the ceiling with her lips slightly parted. Circles of dry milk stained the front of her dress. I had a sudden awful feeling that she was about to howl, but all was quiet except the crackling of the fire. Then she looked down at her hands.

Doc continued. "Emmeline has a gift, a love of literature and learning, and I think she can impart that gift to your children. She'll help them with all the educational skills they would otherwise be lacking out here. She is a brilliant woman."

I don't know why I did it. Maybe I was just so angry at the doctor for talking about her as if she weren't there, or maybe I just felt sorry for her, but as soon as I thought of it, I did it. I went up behind her and put my arms around her shoulders and pressed my face into her collar. Her hands came up and covered my arms, and she tipped her head, catching my face softly in the curve of her neck. I didn't want to let go. I just wanted to stand like that forever, but she looked around at me, and I was forced to look into her dull eyes. "My prairie baby died, Louisa," she said.

"I know."

"Your father dug the grave."

"I helped him."

She pulled me around in front of her. "Could you show me where the flowers are now, prairie girl? For the grave?"

I looked at the doctor for help, but he seemed to be holding his breath. His glistening eyes reflected the fire when Momma opened the stove door and quietly added another chip.

"There are no flowers now, Mrs. Berryman. It's winter."

"Of course." She bobbed her head down and covered her face with a bony hand. "How stupid I've grown." She reached out and rubbed her hands up and down my arms, I guess to warm me, but I felt the gooseflesh grow under her touch.

"I'll show you in the spring, or the summer," I promised.

"And will you come for lessons now?" She looked at me pleadingly.

"Do you want me to?" I asked, hope stealing into my voice.

"Yes," she said. I heard Doc release a long sigh. "Yes,"

she said, a little stronger. "You know, when I see you like this, I remember how much I enjoyed our lessons before. Maybe William is right," she whispered. "Maybe you'll be good for me." She broke off and let go of my arms, staring straight at me but blankly, as if her mind had stepped out of the room.

Momma placed the mugs on the table. "I don't know."

We all looked at her.

"There's just been so much," she said, "and I really don't think it's time. It's too early. . . ."

I suddenly realized Momma was worried about me and Lester. "It'll be fine, Momma. I'd like to go and hear more stories and read and have lessons again."

Lester yelled from under the bed. "I won't go! No! No! No!"

Momma knelt down by him and looked up apologetically at everyone. "It's all right, sweetheart. You don't have to go if you don't want to."

"Why?" the doctor demanded.

"Oh, all that commotion with Paulie and everything was just too much for him. He's very sensitive."

"Paulie?" Mrs. Berryman asked. "What about Paulie?"

There was an awkward silence. Mrs. Berryman didn't remember—the gun, the screaming. I looked down at her skirts and thought of the water pouring out on the ground, and then I was ashamed. The blood came to my face. Lester was crying, and Mrs. Berryman went to kneel down next to Momma.

"Lester?" Mrs. Berryman said. "You don't have to come if you don't want to." There was a silence. "But . . . Lester?"

No answer.

"Can I give you a book to practice on until you feel better? Until you feel like coming?"

"Yes."

She stood then and looked down at Momma. "Very well," she said, and turned as if to walk out.

"Emmeline, your coffee." The doctor stood up nervously.

"I just want to get him a book," she answered.

"Come, Emmeline, sit. Have your coffee, and when we go back we'll pick out a book for Lester. But come now. Sit."

Doc looked at Momma nervously as she poured the steaming coffee into heavy mugs. Her lips were tight, and then she said quietly, "All right, Louisa, you may go if you're sure you want to."

I was the only one who smiled, but not for more than a second.

Chapter Eleven

Even though Momma had agreed to let me go for my lessons the next day, it was raining so hard in the morning that she changed her mind.

"They will understand, Louisa. Surely they don't expect you to walk three miles in this downpour."

"But Momma, she's so sad, and I could go and wear your cape, and—"

"Louisa, go and get the eggs. Tomorrow will be a different day, and if the rain has stopped, you will go."

But the rain hadn't stopped, and the next day, instead of walking to the Berrymans' with an armload of books, I once again collected the night's eggs and milked our cow, Baldy. I was just as wet when I was done with these chores as if I had walked the three miles, and I let everyone know.

Morning was beginning earlier each day, tricking us with its false sense of spring that late January sometimes brought. And the unseasonal rain was another lie. My feet were splattered with cold mud and the single egg I had dropped.

On the third day I awoke listening for rain, and I heard it. Now the rain was also inside, for the roof, good for a day or two, had begun to leak, and Momma had put bowls and pots around, under each drip. I might have enjoyed the uneven music of the drippings, except for knowing that I wouldn't get to the Berrymans' again that day.

But Momma surprised me by having different ideas. She was standing by the stove, furiously beating eggs in the bowl that she held under her arm. It was still dark out, but there was a hint of morning in the air.

"J.T., why don't you take her to the Berrymans' in the wagon for her lessons today?"

He grunted. "I got my chores."

"It's raining, J.T. Surely you could take time just to run her over there. She's so fidgety, and she's driving me crazy with her fretting and nagging."

Poppa was mending his boots with coarse thread and a

giant needle that glinted once in the light of the kerosene lamp. He pulled at it with his teeth. "Maybe."

"J.T.," Momma pleaded.

He turned his head toward her.

"Either you take her over there," she said, "or I will. And if Emmeline Berryman is not in shape for a lesson, I am going to put Louisa in a gunnysack and drown her in the river."

"Momma!" I was sitting up in bed.

"Aha! I thought that would get you up, little snooper." Momma poured the beaten eggs out into the skillet, and they sizzled. "Come on, git up and stop laying abed with one big ear sticking up out of the covers."

I reached to the bottom of my mattress where my day's clothes were and pulled them under the blankets with me, to dress in the warmth of the familiar quilts and covers. My lessons! I was really going for my lessons.

Lester stirred next to me. "I'm staying here," he said, clear and wide-awake, as if he'd been up for hours.

"Lester!" Momma scolded. "I said you could stay home, didn't I? How many times do I have to tell you?"

He disappeared under his blanket and Poppa clucked. "Mercy, woman, you are in a foul mood today." His boot hit the floor, and he struggled to put it on.

Momma's head bent over her eggs in the pan, and she rubbed her hand over her cheek. "Sorry," she mumbled. "It's just this rain, is all. If it doesn't stop soon, I'm going to scream." Her head lifted. "As a matter of fact . . ." She scooped the eggs into the bowl and walked over to one of the pots that was full of water, ready to overflow. She carried it to the door and opened it, letting in a gush of air. She flung the water away from the house, and as she did so, she let out an earsplitting scream, long and loud and awful, that must have skittered for miles over the prairie. She was smiling as she turned to us and closed the door. "There," she said, straightening her collar and setting the pot back down in a puddle beneath the never-ending drip.

Poppa whistled a long, low whistle. "Yes, ma'am," he said. "Sounds like she means business, little snipper. You'd better get your tail out of there and get ready for a little education."

My clothes were on: my leggings, my petticoats, my dress and sweater. I pulled on my shoes that were beside the bed. "Can I do that, Momma?" I asked.

"What?"

"Scream out the door."

"Only if you're emptying a pot of rainwater," Poppa ordered. "It's an old custom in my family, long line of dukes and earls that we are, that we only scream while dumping rain."

I grabbed a pot that was half full on Lester's bed and ran for the door.

"Louisa! Put another pot there. That's a bed!"

But Lester had scooted down to the end of his bed and had opened his mouth to the steady drip.

"Lester!" Momma scolded. "That's disgusting. Sit back." She slid a bowl under the drip and pushed Lester back into his pillow. "Hurry up, Louisa!"

I opened the door and stepped out a ways into the morning chill. I shivered and some water sloshed on my shoe. The edge of the sky was glowing a pale gray, and all around me was the *hush, hush* of prairie rain. I tossed the water out and let out a holler. But it wasn't like Momma's scream at all. It was more like a haaaaa-haaaaa-haaaaa, bursts of noise from the bottom of me somewhere. "Hooooo-hooooo," I continued, listening to it disappear from me, like seeds scattered from a sack.

"Louisa!" I heard Momma call. "Close the door now."

The soddy looked pale yellow as I turned back, and all eyes were on me. "Come on, Lester, your turn."

"I don't wanna," he said. He disappeared under his covers as I replaced the pot on his bed.

Poppa was scooping the eggs onto my dish. "Come on and eat now. And I'll get the wagon. And then you find the gunnysack. It must be around here somewhere. Just in case I have to take you to the Loup."

He smiled at me playfully and bent over his plate, the forkful of eggs disappearing into his mouth.

* * *

Poppa brought the wagon around the front of the soddy and called out to me. I tucked the books under my skirt and ran out, holding them to my stomach.

"Hop in the back," he called, and when I was near him, he threw a huge length of canvas over my head and ordered me to stay under it and keep as dry as I could.

It was dark under the cover, and I felt like I was inside an egg, like a little chick. The rain pounded on the fabric, and I could hear Cap plodding through the mud and grass. There was no sound from Poppa, and I couldn't tell if he was still there. I couldn't tell where we were going. I was just floating along, and the ride seemed to go on and on forever.

The wagon slowed eventually, and I heard Poppa call out, "Doc!"

I peeked from beneath the cover, rain splattering my face. The door to the Berryman soddy opened, and the doc stood there.

"I have brought your wife a student this morning. Are you folks agreeable to such doings today?"

Mrs. Berryman appeared behind him.

"Yes, of course. Send her right in," he answered.

Poppa pulled the canvas off me and a cloud of steam escaped into the air. "If it's still raining at dinnertime, I'll be back for you. Otherwise, walk home yourself. You hear?"

"Yes, Poppa."

I ran to the warm light of the soddy and scooted past Doc Berryman. He stayed there looking out at Poppa.

"J.T.," he called.

"Yes?"

"The roof. It leaks."

"They sure do," I heard Poppa answer. "Ain't it a shame? Have you enough bowls and pots?"

"Yes." The doctor nodded thoughtfully. "Yes, we're doing fine. See you later." He closed the door and turned into the room.

Mrs. Berryman was standing and shivering, wrapped in a heavy shawl. She looked at him hopefully.

"They *all* leak, I guess." He shrugged.

"The books, William. All my books." Her voice whined.

Their soddy was like the inside of mine, and the same music filled it, the steady drip, drip, drip, in china and tin and metal and wood.

"Don't let the muslin fill with water," I said, pointing to the ceiling. "You've got to make more drain spots." I put another pot on the floor, and with a broom handle I touched the end to the muslin on the ceiling where it bulged and hung. Immediately water began to drip from the spot.

Doc looked at it thoughtfully. "Why, thank you, Louise. Another drip. Just what we needed."

"Otherwise the muslin'll tear away from the ceiling."

"Of course. Of course. Is yours leaking like this?"

"Sure." Did he really think it wouldn't? A soddy roof that didn't leak? "And when the rain stops, it'll leak for another two days."

I looked at Mrs. Berryman standing stupidly between two pots that were splashing up on her skirt. She looked soggy all over. "The rain is awful, isn't it, child?"

"Yes, ma'am."

"It makes the cobblestones so slick and dangerous. Why, just yesterday I went out for some fresh fish, and I got two blocks, and I had to turn around and come home. It was treacherous."

Doc hustled me over to the stove. "Here, sit down, here, by the nice warm fire. See that? Isn't it dry and warm right here? Come, darling, your student is here. Let's begin the lesson."

Mrs. Berryman gathered up her skirts and stepped over the pot as water splashed on top of her head and ran down past her ears. "Of course," she said. "Let's begin, shall we?"

And so it went. I couldn't decide which was worse, being home with Momma and Poppa and Lester all day in a closed-up soddy, or being stuck all day with Doc and Mrs. Berryman. I couldn't sit at the table to write because of the dripping water, so all we did was read. She read to me for a while, which was nice, but her voice grew hoarse, and she coughed. Her body whistled as she breathed.

"Where's Lester?" she asked. She looked around the

room as if she suddenly realized he wasn't with us.

"He didn't want to come, ma'am. He's so foolish shy and silly. I say to him, 'Lester, you got to stop this and start talking to people and making friends when you can, seeing as how there are so few opportunities.' "

She was staring at me and not seeing me. I rambled on nervously. " 'You know,' I tell him, 'you can't go on the rest of your life like this, Lester. You gotta be like everybody else and stop all this nonsense.' "

"Louisa?" Her eyes were focused on mine.

"Yes?"

"Let him be what he is, you hear?"

"But Mrs. Berryman—"

"Louisa," she said firmly.

"Yes?"

"He may not be ready for all you want him to be. Just leave him to grow at his own pace, and maybe someday he'll come around."

I looked at her curiously. That dress, once violet and beautiful—was it that first dress—was faded from drying in the bright sun week after week. Doc Berryman coughed.

"But Lester needs a little bit of pushing, ma'am, or he won't never amount to nothing."

"I don't think pushing will do anything but trouble him more. He has to grow on his own. Can you make a sunflower hurry?"

"No, ma'am, but Lester ain't—"

"Can you make a calf give milk?"

"Well—"

"Or the sun come up a bit early because you've got a lot of things to do that day?"

"No, ma'am, but how about this year's Independence Day celebration? Lester's gotta say something for the recitations. Everybody does. Poppa says he can't sit in the wagon all day this year. That it's about time for him to start acting his age."

Mrs. Berryman rubbed her hands over her eyes and sighed. "Poor Lester. Leave him be, sweetheart. Here." She handed me the book that was in her lap. "Read to me awhile now. Let me hear how you've progressed."

I hadn't read but one page when she was slumped over, sound asleep, her hands finally limp and still in her lap. Then I grew hoarse, too, my throat dry and aching, and I began to read silently, just to myself. Doc lay stretched out on the bed, and by his deep breathing I knew that he, too, was asleep. And there I was in this soddy, pots and bowls filling up all around me, and everyone was asleep.

I emptied a pot outside once in a while, looking toward home to see if Poppa was coming for me yet. I thought of yelling as the water tossed through the air—maybe Poppa would hear me—but I was quiet. I was sorry I had come.

I set to work copying the eagle poem on a piece of paper in my lap. I would read it at the Independence Day celebration. I would memorize it and read it without a paper in front of me, the way a minister recites things from the Bible.

Balancing the book and a small piece of paper in my lap, I wrote with small tight letters and copied the poem to take home. Doc rose up after a while and emptied a few pots himself, coming back in wetter and more tired-looking. "Louise, I'm going to the stable. I'll be back in a little while." He looked at his wife. "I guess this was a mistake." He put on his hat, slipped into his heavy coat and then out the door.

I missed Lester. I added some chips to the fire, and the noise woke Mrs. Berryman. She looked up at me as if she didn't know who I was. Her eyes grew. She looked around the room and gasped. "My books," she whispered. "My books. My God."

She began to rush around the room, gathering up the books into her arms. She kicked over a bowl and didn't stop to fix it. I watched her, not knowing what to do.

"My books, my books," she kept saying over and over. She pushed a bucket off her trunk and it splattered to the floor and rolled across the room. She opened the trunk full of clothes and fabrics, and began wrapping her books methodically, one at a time, in the garments. She would wrap a book carefully, tucking in loose edges, and then place it on the wet table.

"Mrs. Berryman," I whispered. No answer. I wished Doc hadn't gone out. It seemed a crazy thing to do, wrap up books like that, but she kept doing it. Then she pushed a bowl off the table onto the floor. It splashed and broke. A broken bowl was enough to make Momma upset for days, but Mrs. Berryman didn't even notice. She kept wrapping the books and piling them up. Water dripped from the ceiling, splattering on the pile, making a strange new note in the room.

I sat in the chair and watched, not sure what to do. If only Doc would come back in. She was smiling, maybe, or baring her teeth. She coughed and wiped her nose on her fingers.

Maybe he would hear me if I yelled. "Doc!" At the top of my lungs. No one answered, and she didn't seem to notice me. "Doc!"

There were more books than garments, so when the trunk was empty of fabrics and clothes, she just piled the other books on top of the wrapped books, and then she pulled a chair over to the table. She stepped up on the chair and climbed on top of the pile, dropping her skirt over them, like a brood hen. I ran out the door.

I tore through the torrents of freezing rain to the stable, where I found Doc feeding his horse and talking soothingly to it. He spun around at the sound of my voice. I was breathless.

"Come quick! She's on the table with all her books!"

He held his head in both hands. There was nowhere for me to run. Where was Poppa? Where was Cap? I wanted to go home.

I felt him brush past me, and the barn was so cold, I

followed him back to the soddy. He was slipping his arms around her. "Come to bed, Emmeline. Come."

"Get away!" she screamed, hitting him in the throat with her elbow.

He backed away and choked. "Emmeline, please, please, that's enough. I can't stand this anymore. . . . I can't . . . please . . . for God's sake." He wrestled her off the table, and the books clattered to the floor, falling in puddles. The clothes were wet, the pages were open, everything was wet and soggy.

"The books! The books!" she was screeching. "They'll die! They'll die from this rain!"

I stood in the doorway, my hands over my mouth, shivering and frightened. When he reached across and slapped her face, I closed my eyes and began to cry. But when I opened my eyes, she was quiet and in the big bed, and Doc was positioning yet another pot by her feet to catch the rain.

"I want to go home," I said, sobbing.

"Home," she echoed.

"It's all right," he said. "You're all right now." He came to me and held out his hand, the hand that had just hit Mrs. Berryman, beautiful Mrs. Berryman in her violet dress.

"Sit by the fire, child. Your father will be here shortly."

I walked next to him to the stove, and we both sat there staring into the fire, listening to the crackling until, what seemed like hours later, we heard the sound of Poppa coming for me.

I jumped into the wagon and rode home under the canvas. I had forgotten to take a book, but carefully I reached up into my sleeve and felt for my paper. It was there, dry and folded small. I knew the first two lines already, and I said them over and over to myself to keep from getting scared, to keep from crying in a place where Poppa couldn't get ahold of me and hug me to him.

> "*He clasps the crag with crooked hands;*
> *Close to the sun in lonely lands . . .*
> *He clasps the crag with crooked hands;*
> *Close to the sun in lonely lands . . .*"

Chapter Twelve

I was piecing together scraps of fabric for my first quilt. Tiny shreds of loose skin dotted the tip of my finger from the needle, because Momma was using the only thimble. My hands felt fat and awkward. Lester was out with Poppa in the new snow, checking on everything and feeding the animals.

It was very quiet. The soddy was muffled under a quilt

of heavy snow; everything seemed soft and still. We could hear Poppa's voice in the barn. Even in the night sometimes we could hear Cap paw the ground or snort. The world was close and snug. Momma threw another chip on the fire and closed the stove quietly.

"Momma, do you know what's a hot house-flower?"

"Well, in some places they have these heated buildings made out of glass—the walls, the roofs—so that the sun can get in all day long, and they grow flowers and plants in there that normally wouldn't be able to grow anywhere else, or at that season of the year. Why? Where did you ever hear that?"

"Oh, I heard Doc say that that's what Mrs. Berryman was, a hot house-flower. I thought he meant a flower that would burn in the house."

"Doc said that?" Momma frowned. "He hardly gave that woman a chance, did he?"

Suddenly there was stomping and hollering outside. We hadn't even heard a wagon approach, the snow did such peculiar things with sounds, but when we looked outside, we could see Carney Whitfield talking to Poppa. They seemed to explode into the soddy.

"I hear it's the worst thing anyone's seen around here. A real mess." He was huffing and puffing big clouds of steam. Poppa looked at Momma.

"There's been a serious train wreck, Clara. Over at Grand Island. With the snow and ice, a train derailed, turning over cars and everything, and there's lots of injuries, and—"

Mr. Whitfield interrupted him. "And another thing they're worried about now is all those supplies lying around all over the snow. There's some worry that the few bands of Indians left roaming around might just come and take whatever they please. Nobody wants any trouble. But it's real bad, nobody to defend it, nobody to carry the bodies—the dead and injured—to safety."

"Dear God." Momma pressed her fingers to her mouth. "What can we do?"

Carney Whitfield stomped the snow off his boots onto her rug. "Well, I'm going over to get Doc and take him over there, and we'll see what's what."

"I'm going, too, Clara." Poppa took his gun off the wall and began pulling pouches and powder flasks out of drawers as he rushed around the soddy.

Momma grabbed her wrap. "Children, put on your coats."

Poppa stared at her. "Clara, don't be ridiculous. You can't go. You stay here with the children."

Momma tossed Lester's hat at him and blew out the flame in the lamp near where we were sewing. "I mean to go to Doc's with you. He can't leave Emmeline alone, I don't imagine. I'll bring her back here."

Poppa nodded agreement and left with Mr. Whitfield to harness up the wagon and go get the doctor. Lester followed after Momma. "Are you leaving, Momma? Where

is Poppa going? To a railroad? And what about the Indians?"

"Lester, Lester, don't fret yourself none. We're just
going over to see Mrs. Berryman." She buttoned his coat
quickly, jerking his arms and body as she pulled it tightly
around him.

"Is Poppa going to fight Indians, Momma?" I asked,
starting to feel a vast pit open up in my stomach.

She glared at me. "Louisa, I will do the worrying, if
you don't mind. Don't go imagining things. Poppa's going
to help at a train wreck that happened in Grand Island;
that's all there is to it. Now put your imagination to rest
and go git in the wagon."

Lester and I held hands and ran out to the wagon. I
remember watching Poppa as if I would never see him
again, and I could see so little of him, in his heavy coat
and the scarf wrapped around his neck and head. But I
memorized how he always sat in the wagon seat, one hand
on his knee, as he waited for Momma to climb up beside
him. She turned and tossed a blanket over us, and we
snuggled together, watching our breaths escape in small
clouds as Poppa made Cap hurry through the brittle snow.
Our teeth rattled, and we jiggled and banged around till
I couldn't stand it anymore. Leaving the warmth of the
blanket, I knelt up and looked out at the white, stark
prairie slipping by.

There were snowdrifts where there had never been swells

before, the snow being easier and more willing for the wind than prairie grass and dust. Poppa pointed out to the horizon where a low cloud of steam seemed to sit in one spot for no reason. "Know what that is?" he called back to us. "That's a lost herd of cattle, huddled together for warmth." He kept gazing out at it. "Wish I had time to stop. Wonder who they belong to?"

"They got a lot more sense than people," Momma said. "Foolish people spread out all over, out of touch, in separate little corners with no one for miles and miles around."

Poppa snapped the reins angrily. "Don't start that now, Clara. I have no heart to argue about the loneliness of farm life and how you'd prefer to be all huddled up with a bunch of cozy friends."

Momma didn't say a word. I had never heard this talk before. Was Momma lonely, too? I watched the cloud over the lost herd until it disappeared from view. Up ahead, Mr. Whitfield drove his wagon along, and he was out of the wagon and at the door of the Berrymans' soddy when we pulled up alongside him.

"Doc! Doc!" he was yelling. The door flew open, and Doc's haggard face looked out. "There's been a really bad train wreck down by Grand Island. Lots of wounded, and lots of trouble, maybe, with Indians if we don't get some help down there."

"I'll be right with you," Doc said, and he disappeared

into his soddy. Momma got down and went in after him. We followed.

"Doc, I'll take Emmeline home with me," she was saying. Mrs. Berryman was sitting on a chair before the stove, her shawl wrapped around her shoulders, her face loose and staring at the heat rising off the top. Slowly, as if in a trance, she bent forward, picked up a chip and threw it in the fire. She sat back again and folded her hands in her lap. She didn't even look up at us. Momma stood there uncertainly.

"She'll be all right," the doc said, pulling on his coat.

Momma stared at him. "All alone?"

He stood looking at his wife, his arms hanging limply at his sides. "She sits. She keeps the fire going. She eats when she's hungry. She stares. She doesn't even know if I'm here or not."

"But surely you can't mean to leave her all alone here. She's so frightened to be alone."

"It doesn't seem to matter to her anymore." He shrugged. And I suddenly realized how sad he looked.

Poppa opened the door and shouted in, "Come on, Doc, we'd better get moving. We've got a long ride ahead of us. Clara . . ."

She looked up at him and walked slowly to the door.

"I'm leaving the wagon with you for whatever you decide. We'll take Doc's wagon and his horse, and Carney's."

Momma reached out and touched his sleeve. "Careful, J.T."

Poppa nodded and turned from her, and I watched Doc reach up and take down the rifle that hung next to the door.

"I'll have something hot for you to eat when you come back," Momma called after them, and then she closed the door quietly, as if a baby were sleeping.

I went and stood near Mrs. Berryman and put my hand on the back of her chair. It had been our chair, and there was a little knob on the back. Momma used to sit in it to nurse Delilah, and I would wrap my fingers around the knob and lean my chin on it to watch and listen to my sister's gurgling noises. Now I just touched my finger to the knob with uncertainty. Mrs. Berryman didn't move.

Momma brought her the heavy red-colored coat that hung on the wall. "Emmeline?" she said quietly.

But Mrs. Berryman remained staring at the stove.

"Emmeline, Doc has to go away for a day or two, and I'm going to take you home with me for the time being."

She remained perfectly still.

"Emmeline, dear, put your coat on." Momma moved toward her with the coat held up; Mrs. Berryman held up her hand to push it away.

"Emmeline, please, be reasonable. Come with me."

"Go home" was all she said.

"But you'll be alone. Doc had to go help out in an

emergency out at Grand Island. Come with me, now."

Mrs. Berryman turned and looked at Momma. The skin on her face was dry and cracked. There seemed to be chalky film over her cheeks. Her hair was pulled back from her face severely, as if there were no more life in it.

"I'm staying here," she said firmly. Momma backed off a step.

"I can't stay here with you, Emmeline. I have the children and the chores at home."

"I want to stay here alone," she answered. Her gaze went back to the stove, as if dismissing all of us. Then I noticed how none of the books were in sight. Not a single book was on the shelves or in the boxes, or on the table, or on the bed. But under the stove were some torn pages— bent, ripped pages that in my horror reminded me of tiny pieces of leftover kindling, or little pieces of chips broken off and left to be swept up and dumped into the stove.

Momma was looking at us as if for an answer. I stood near her, and Lester hung back in the shadow of the doorway.

"Well, I have to leave. But I'll come back tomorrow and check on you."

Not a word.

Momma put her hand on Mrs. Berryman's shoulder, but there was no response. All the nervous twittering and shaking was gone. She seemed as hard and as still as the soddy itself.

"Well . . ." Momma backed up and reached her hands out to us. She hesitated in the doorway, holding each of us by a hand and looking back into the room. Maybe she never should have left Mrs. Berryman that way, but there was no way she could have known that then. It was the same thing I would have done, I guess, had I been Momma. She asked Mrs. Berryman to come and got, in return, a sure and certain no.

But Momma never believed she had done all she could to persuade her. She later said that she was so worried herself about Poppa she wasn't thinking straight, and that if she had been thinking straight, she just would have insisted; that's all there was to it.

Momma drove the wagon back to the soddy slower than Poppa had done, and we stopped a minute to gaze out at the lost herd. "Someone in the middle there is nice and warm, that's for sure," Momma said.

"How about the ones on the outside?" Lester asked.

Momma frowned, snapped the reins and pulled away.

"How about them?" Lester asked again.

"They'll probably die, son. Frozen solid."

Chapter Thirteen

Momma had a small calendar tacked to the inside of the soddy door, and all through the long winter we would check it, measuring how far off spring was, and we could hope for the comfort we knew always came.

But comfort was a long way off. Easter was in April, and that was my guide. With Easter would come an easing of the cold, hard winter, and before the heat of summer would be a magic time of sweater days and chilly nights of star-burdened skies calling to be seen.

When we returned from the Berrymans' that day, I stood looking at the calendar. Again I counted. Easter was seventy-three days away. And then Independence Day.

"Momma, where is the Fourth of July celebration this year?"

Momma had hung her coat up and was rebuilding the fire, poking it and adding another chip and some twigs collected from the creek.

"Oh, I think Pru said it would be in Central City this year. Yes, Central City, I believe."

"Will we go and sleep in the wagon again? Under the stars?"

"Yes, we might."

"Can we bring the Berrymans with us?"

"Louisa, please! You have two million questions to torment me with. Ask me the week before, not now. July is an eternity away."

"But I need to know about memorizing my poem."

"Louisa." She turned her tired eyes on me. "Practice your poem and stop worrying about everything. Please."

"But Momma—"

"If you want to worry about something, worry about your father out risking his neck at the train wreck with crazy Indians around, and God knows what—" Momma put her hands to her face. "Oh, dear God, listen to me. Children, children, I'm so tired. Just leave me alone and let me get some chores done."

"Are the Indians gonna try to kill Poppa?" Lester asked.

"Of course not, Lester. Poppa is going to help out, and as soon as everything is under control, he'll be back with Doc and Mr. Whitfield, and we'll have a nice hot dinner celebration. How about if we make some popcorn now? How would that be?"

Lester went and got the jar full of dried corn, and Momma pulled out the pot with the heavy lid on it. "Louisa, go get the butter, and hurry back."

I hadn't even taken my coat off yet, so I stepped outside as I was, the day weighing down on me, my face suddenly tight with cold and sharpness.

The cellar, always so cool in the summer, felt warm now as I went down the dirt steps and scooped out a bowl of rich butter from the wooden keg. I checked the crate that had once held red polished apples from Philadelphia, but they were all gone. I popped a dry raisin into my mouth, and then another. What if Poppa never came back? What if he was shot and no one could take care of him, because they were too busy with all the other people on the train? I worked up a good sob, thinking about Poppa getting killed and what would we do without him, and yet somehow that didn't really seem possible. Poppa would always come back. I knew he was always there, just like

I knew the sun would come up tomorrow and that Easter would bring warmer weather. In the midst of my tears and coughing sobs, I remembered the sight of the papers under Mrs. Berryman's stove, and then I let loose with my real sorrow, the uneasiness I had been feeling ever since we were there. I felt inside my stocking. It was still there, not stiff anymore, but the letters were still clear, even though I didn't need it anymore. I had the entire poem memorized.

I sat awhile until I was all cried out, and then I climbed back up into the cold day. I stood locked to the spot. Off in the distance, shadowed by the bright snow and the distant gray sky, came two figures, formless and huge. I bolted for the soddy and burst in the door.

"Momma! Momma! Indians are coming!"

"Oh, no," Momma said, and I saw her eyes go to the hooks above the door where Poppa's gun no longer hung. Lester screamed and began hanging on to her skirts as if to be lifted in her arms like a baby.

"Lester!" She grabbed him by the shoulders and put her face right near his. "Don't do this. We have to be calm and polite, and they'll go away once they've had something to eat. Is that clear?" He sobbed louder. She shook him angrily. "Lester, stop it!"

"Momma, Momma," he sobbed, and she slapped him across the face the way I had seen Doc hit his wife. But Momma immediately hugged Lester to her, winding her fingers through his strawlike hair. "Sh, sh, now, child."

I peered out the window in the direction they had been coming from. "Maybe they'll just pass on, Momma." But we heard their voices then, low and gruff. Lester flew under the bed, disappearing like a cricket.

The unlocked door opened, and the Indians entered. There were two of them, shabby and sunken-looking men, dressed in a hodgepodge of Indian clothes and farmer clothes. One wore layers of heavy red undershirts like Poppa's, with three buttons, but the buttons were gone and hanging from the buttonholes were strings of tiny river conch shells. The other Indian wore heavy overalls that seemed new, and on his feet were ragged shoes of rough leather decorated with thin shells that were broken and splintered.

Momma stood near the stove and watched, her face drained of expression. The Indians were between her and me, and I watched as she forced a smile on her face. "Good afternoon," she said clearly and politely, as if Pru Whitfield had just stopped in for a cup of coffee and some quilting.

The Indian in the overalls looked around the room as the other Indian closed the door behind them. They saw Momma at the stove, me at the window and our small soddy, the table, the beds and the few chairs. They said a few words in what I knew to be Lakota and pointed at the stove. They threw their blankets on the table, and suddenly it smelled as if we had just brought Cap into the house. Momma backed up and banged awkwardly into the wall, the popcorn pot still in her hand.

"Yes, of course," she answered, nodding hard, as if to assure them that she would give them food. With trembling hands, she pulled bread out of the larder, and a long knife. She always cut bread on the table, but with the blankets there now, she placed the bread on the warm stove and cut it roughly into two large pieces. She handed a piece to each of them. They ate immediately, grunting and tearing like dogs with meaty bones.

One spoke again, this time pointing at the pot she had put down. Momma stood looking at them. It was as if she were on a stage, and they were making her perform. She turned her back and pulled from the cupboard some jars of food that she had canned during the summer. She put the popcorn pot on the stove and began emptying the jars into it—canned green beans, canned corn, chicken broth. "Louisa, go and get a large piece of the ham that's in the cellar."

The men turned and looked at me, and I scooted out the door. I felt as if I were floating in the air, watching myself do all the things I had to do, watching Momma alone in the house, cooking for the Indians. Last time Poppa had been home. Last time the gun had been hanging over the door. I tucked the piece of ham under my coat and ran back to Momma. They were all as I had left them, but now the Indians were sitting on the floor near the stove. I approached cautiously, holding the meat before me.

Momma accepted it and held me with her eyes. "Sit down now and just be still and quiet, and soon we'll be alone again. Just be calm and wait."

I nodded and sat down beside the table with the heaped blankets, easing my own coat off in the warmth. The Indians talked to each other, strange words I didn't know, and strange sounds that I had heard only once before. I sat and listened, and watched Momma as she browned the meat, and the wonderful smell filled the soddy.

I concentrated on not moving a single muscle, not twitching or changing position even once. I just sat as still as a sleeping horse.

"Louisa." Momma was looking at me. "Get me two big bowls."

As I collected the bowls in my arms, I heard Lester sniff. He was under the bed, still, never even saw the Indians, and they didn't know he was there. There was no way for me to comfort him or say a word to him. And it occurred to me that, later, he would not have a story to tell like I would, about the day the Indians came when Poppa wasn't here.

"Come on out . . ." I began quietly.

"Leave him be," Momma said low and calm. "Just leave him be right where he is." She said it almost as if she were talking out loud to herself. One Indian coughed loudly with a peculiar rattle and spit on the floor. Momma's eyes widened in warning to me, and I sat back down on the seat and watched her scoop the food into the bowls. She used it all up on them, all of it in two bowls, two Indians, not a thing left for us, and the air smelled like beautiful ham and soup.

She stood with her hands folded at her waist and watched as they slurped the food with the bowls to their faces and their fingers in the vegetables.

When their bowls were nearly empty, Lester made this Godawful noise under the bed that scared even me, and I knew he was there. I guess it was a sob or a moan, mixed up with a little terror, but it sounded for all the world like a wild animal, and the Indians stood suddenly, throwing the bowls off their laps and drawing their knives. The larger and darker of them lunged for the bed with his knife in the lead, his other hand in a fist. Momma lunged after him and screamed, "No! No!" The other Indian grabbed Momma and held her back. The dark one reached under, and I heard the wild squeal of a trapped animal. He pulled Lester out by a foot, squirming and kicking. He turned to his friend with Lester held out before him, hanging by one leg. Momma had begun to cry. Lester's upside-down face was red and horrified, and I can still see those tears running up his forehead and dripping onto the floor from strands of darkened hair.

My arms buzzed with terror. My ears rang, and my

whole body was rigid, ready to tear out the door. But the Indian holding Lester began to laugh, showing his brown, even teeth. His friend laughed, and Momma stood frozen. Lester grew limp, and the Indian flipped him up as I had seen Poppa do to him so many times when they wrestled. He held Lester in his arms and looked at him closely. In the embrace, his knife was still held in his hand, but he held it away from Lester, its shiny glint catching the glow of the lamp.

"Wolf," the Indian said in English. Lester stared at him. "Wolf," he repeated, tapping Lester's chest with a long finger. Then he set Lester down and turned and spoke to his friend in Lakota; he mimed himself lunging under the bed. "Ah!" He held his arm up as if Lester still hung from his hand. "Yellow Wolf."

"I think he's saying he thought you were a wolf under the bed," Momma said, reaching out to Lester, who immediately went into her arms and held fast. The Indian reached out and clasped a bit of Lester's hair in his fingers. His knife appeared, my breath caught, but it was all over in an instant. He cut a clump of Lester's hair and held it out to his friend. "Yellow Wolf."

"I think he's calling you Yellow Wolf, Lester," I said. "You know, like an Indian name."

The back of Lester's neck was as rigid as a willow branch, little tendons protruding, so vulnerable and clear.

The Indian turned to Momma, and she glared at him

defiantly. Suddenly I was scared because I realized her politeness had worn out. Her mouth was in a tight line; her eyes were mean. They looked at each other a long time, seemed like hours, but maybe not. I knew the fire suddenly sounded very loud, and the smell of the Indians began to take over again now that the ham was eaten and gone. Momma stood glaring at him, and he slid his knife back into its sheath slowly and turned to his friend. They spoke. They lifted their blankets off the table and after shaking them out, drew them about their shoulders. They looked at Momma, nodded, grunted. "Hakahe," one said, and as simply as they had come, they left, leaving the door ajar.

Momma ran to the door and shut it tight, bolted it, and leaned back against it, her chest heaving with new breath, her eyes searching wildly around the soddy. We froze. We were silent, listening to the sounds, not knowing what we would hear, but when we did hear something, we knew what we'd been waiting for. There were muffled sounds in the barn, and then the soft clopping of Cap's hooves in the snow. They were taking Cap with them. As surely as they had helped themselves to our ham, they were leaving with our horse.

"Cap, Momma! They're taking Cap!"

Momma held her finger to her lips to silence me. She listened, her fingers spreading over her mouth, her nose and then her eyes. The steps faded away into a muffled distance. I ran to the window and watched them disappear into the cold winter sun. Lester sniffed and wiped his nose on the back of his sleeve.

"Are they gone?" he asked.

"Looks like," I answered.

Lester stood there, and like a sky suddenly turning pink in an instant at sunrise, a smile spread across his face. "Did you see that, Louisa?" he asked. "Held me upside down by one foot."

I stared at him in disbelief.

"Called me Yellow Wolf, he did."

I looked at the patch of his hair that was cut so crooked where the Indian had taken a piece. His left eyebrow showed darkly, like a finely drawn line protecting his small gray eye. He had a look of permanent surprise.

And then Momma began to scrub down the table, wetting it and rubbing it, drying and rubbing and drying, over and over with a look of disgust and fury on her face. "Awful savages," she muttered. "All that good ham . . . touched my children . . ."

It was beginning to grow dark out. The Indians were nowhere to be seen, and Cap was gone forever, off to who-knows-what kinds of adventures. I was afraid to go check on the chickens or make sure Baldy was secure for the night. When Poppa wasn't home that was usually my job, but Momma threw on her shawl toward night. "Louisa, bolt the door, and open it when I return."

"They're gone, Momma. You don't have to—"

"Bolt the door, child."

I added more chips to the fire, stirred it around and stared down into the embers, a glowing otherworld of brilliant orange and heat, reminding me somehow of another land of people, huddled together in comfort and company.

The wind picked up that night, howling and tearing, and I wondered about Cap as I layd there, wrapped in covers and nightgowns and extra layers of socks. The soddy was still. Lester breathed noisily, and I couldn't hear Momma in her and Poppa's big bed, but I knew she was alone and listening as I was for the sound of a returning wagon. But Poppa didn't come back that night.

Chapter Fourteen

I awoke to the sound of Momma's voice the next morning. It was dark, early, and the sound of the wind was
still whipping at the house. "Oh, my God!" she said.
She was sitting in her bed with the blankets pulled up to
her with tense hands.

"What's the matter, Momma?" I didn't dare sit up. The
air in the soddy was brutally cold.

"Emmeline," she said. "Emmeline's been all alone, and—"

The Indians. I knew.

She slipped out of bed and pulled on her heavy dress, her arms slipping in jerks down the sleeves, her head emerging from the collar. She threw chips in the fire as she buttoned her dress, then slapped her arms and rubbed her hands together for warmth.

"Bring your clothes over here and get dressed. We have to get over to the Berrymans' right away and check on her. Poor woman is probably frightened right out of her wits."

I scooped up my clothes and ran to sit by the fire, right where the Indians had been.

"Which way were they going yesterday, Louisa?"

I remembered. "Toward the Berrymans'."

Hurriedly she stirred a pot of cold oatmeal. "Watch this, Louisa, while I go milk Baldy. Get up, Lester. We have to check on Mrs. Berryman to see if the Indians paid her a call."

He scooted in beside me by the fire, and in a mad rush pulled on his heavy shirt and his overalls over that. He knelt before the stove and held his arms around it as if to hug it, but from an inch away.

"You'll set yourself aflame," I warned, stirring the oatmeal as it crackled against the heat of the pan. But he sat there, ignoring me. He never listened to sense.

When Momma came back she stomped the snow from her feet in the doorway. "I forgot that Cap is gone, children. We're going to have to walk to the Berrymans'. Put on extra clothes, all you have." She looked at me a moment. "Or would you rather wait here until I get back?"

"No!" Lester shouted, running to get more clothes. "We'll go with you."

Momma dished out the oatmeal, and we sat quietly, no one saying a word, slowly warming on the inside, thinking about how cold it was, and listening to the wind gusting with window-rattling force now and then.

How many times had we walked to the Berrymans'? I knew the way by heart and in my sleep, but with the drifts of old snow still being pushed about by the driving winds, it wasn't so easy. The dull glow in the sky kept us right as we bent into the wind and plodded along, single file.

First my toes failed, searing pain bending and crackling them as if they were brittle branches. My fingers grew numb, and as my scarf kept falling away from my face, my nose grew cold, my cheeks crusted with frozen tears. I felt in my mind to see if any part of me at all was warm, but there seemed to be no warmth anywhere. I remembered the mist of warmth that hung on the prairie over the herd of cattle. No such cloud protected us.

When we arrived at the soddy, Momma was carrying Lester and he was sobbing, and I was angry at him. The door to the soddy stood wide open, and Momma hesitated in the doorway. "Dear God," she whispered. "Where can she be?"

Inside there was not a sign of life. The fire was out, the lamp was out, and Emmeline's coat was hung on the hook where it always was.

"Emmeline?" Momma called, uneasily.

Dead silence.

Lester slid down out of Momma's arms. "Come, children, let me build a fire. Come sit here and warm up."

Lester walked cautiously to the bed and peered under. "Mrs. Berryman?" he whispered.

Momma started a fire in the stove and slammed the door shut. Her hands were trembling and red with cold. We followed her out the door. Somehow she offered more safety and warmth than any fire, and I guess we just didn't want to let her out of our sight.

She looked at the ground. "It's so hard to tell," she said softly. "The snow is old and packed."

Lester peeked around the side of the soddy and lumbered off on his own. I started to go after him, scanning the now-bright horizon for signs of . . . what? Mrs. Berryman? Poppa? Indians?

Lester screamed a shattering scream at that instant, and Momma rushed past me, nearly knocking me down. I went after her. In less than a breath, it seemed, Momma had picked Lester up and tossed him back toward the front of the soddy. In the same instant, she shoved me away. But not before I saw.

Mrs. Berryman was sitting in the snow, and this is the second picture I will always have of her in my mind—Emmeline was frozen. She had on only a gingham dress, and her shawl was lying around her skirt. I can't remember much else except her hands and face frozen in great horror. Her fingers were extended, stiff icicles of white flesh, and her face, finely coated with white frost, was captured in a ghastly, silent scream that must have locked her face long before the cold did.

"Get in the soddy, Louisa! Look after your brother. Louisa, now!"

I could barely take my eyes off her, sitting there, crusted to the ground, but Momma seized my shoulders and whipped me around.

Lester was sitting near the fire, and he looked up as I entered the room. He didn't say anything. He just looked at me. He had seen. He knew.

The stove was crackling with warmth, steam rising off it. I sat near Lester, pulled my chair right up close to him, for warmth maybe, maybe not. We felt ghosts in the air.

But then Momma came to the door. "Louisa." Her face was ashen. "I need your help. We must get Mrs. Berryman back into the house. Thank God there were no wolves last night."

I rose to follow, but she didn't move. She just stood there in the doorway, and when I approached she held me to her, my head nearly resting on her shoulder, I had grown so tall over the winter. "Louisa, this is no job for a child." Her eyes met mine and she pushed a strand of hair away from my brow. "Now you must be a woman and help me. Can you do that?"

I nodded hard. But what? What would she have me do?

I followed Momma around the side of the soddy, where in the summer Mrs. Berryman had talked of planting a vegetable garden or flowers. She was still there, rigid and lifeless. Momma had thrown the shawl over her face, but her arms still stuck out.

"Take an arm" was all Momma said, and carefully we approached. She was stiff. Her arm wouldn't lower. I slipped my gloved hands under her, remembering how she had worn gloves to go chip picking, and feeling grateful now that I had heavy mittens between me and her.

Momma and I tried to lift her, but she fell forward, heavy and awkward. "See if you can take a leg, too," Momma said through her scarf. We held her by an arm and a leg and carried her between us like a heavy chair being moved indoors, the summer evening over and done.

Lester sat with his back to the door, his hair silhouetted in the light, perfect with fear. It stuck up all around in a wild static. He didn't look.

We carried her low between us, she was so heavy. And she was too heavy to lift onto the bed. We placed her on the floor next to it. She fell on her back, the dirt floor she hated so much softening her fall. Her hands and legs stuck up grotesquely. The scarf fell from her face, and I looked away.

"Poor woman," Momma was saying. "Poor, poor Emmeline." Momma pulled the heavy quilts and comforter off the bed and covered Mrs. Berryman. She wouldn't lie flat.

"Warm up a bit, children, and then we'll go home . . . and wait for Poppa and the doc."

"Home? Can we leave Mrs. Berryman like this?"

Momma passed her hand down my arm and sighed. "There's nothing more that can be done, sweetheart. That's it for now. I don't know what else to do." She turned and looked at the covered form on the floor. "Doc will have to decide what happens next. He'll be back soon."

"Is Mrs. Berryman dead, Momma?" Lester didn't take his eyes off the fire. A small muscle on his cheek rose and disappeared again and again.

"Yes, Lester." Momma pulled the chair up near the stove and slipped off her heavy shoes. "Mrs. Berryman is dead."

"Do you think the Indians got her?" I whispered.

"Oh, no. I think she was just frightened and ran out, and . . . and . . . I don't know . . . just fell apart."

We started back once we had warmed our clothes and thawed out our fingers and toes a bit. Momma bolted the door tightly from the outside and led the way back home.

Chapter Fifteen

Easter came, then warmth, and then July.

I had long since lost the paper that had my poem on it, but I no longer needed it. It was memorized in my mind like my momma's voice.

The day before Independence Day, Poppa readied the wagon and we all started off toward Central City. The prairies were bright green, and the sky could not have been any bluer. We rode in silence, Taffy's eager young hooves louder and racier than I ever remembered Cap's. She seemed like me, seemed like she wanted to shake off her harness, run wild and meet us up ahead.

Momma had packed loads of food, and Lester and I sneaked bits and pieces of different dishes as we sat there, inching our hands up under the cover without making a sound, and then stuffing whatever morsel we could find into our mouths.

The folks in town had set up a tent for the speeches and recitations, and all over there were chairs and wagons and people and kids racing about. A small band was making music, and a group of people stood around them, clapping their hands and tapping their feet. Lester didn't hide, but he sat real still and watched as we rode into the midst of the activity. People had put their wagons all around for sleeping that night, and for socializing and sharing the year's stories. We rode among them slowly, looking for a place for our own wagon.

Poppa was greeted by quite a few men who knew him by name. "J.T.!" they'd call, and Poppa would nod, wave and smile. "Howard, how are you?" "Jesse, good to see you." Momma sat so straight and proud in her best pale gingham dress. Doc had given her all the beautiful dresses, but Momma said she could never wear them and had begun tearing them apart for quilts and piecing.

"Momma! Poppa! Look!" I stood up in the wagon, barely

able to contain myself. There, off to the side, was a big old tree, and tied on just about every branch was a red, white or blue streamer. Beneath the tree, in its precious shade, were dozens of spindly wooden easels, and on each one was a photoprint, I could tell. Shiny gray pictures. Solomon Butcher's pictures! And one would be a picture of me with everybody in front of our soddy. "Momma, oh, let me go see! I have to see!"

Poppa drew the wagon to a halt, and he looked at Momma. "Go ahead," he said. "You go with the children, and I'll meet you there as soon as I take care of the wagon."

She smiled at him and then at us. "All right," she said, "but remember, no running wild, and don't get lost."

Lester and I were out of the wagon like lightning, and we raced each other to the tree. There were only a few people looking at the photographs, and I looked around for Mr. Butcher, but he was nowhere in sight. Had he kept his promise? Had he made that picture of us? Lester slid his hand into mine, and very slowly we peered at each picture, searching.

First, there was a picture of a family in front of a small soddy, smaller than ours, but the little boy in the picture was holding a giant fiddle at his side. It was twice as big as he was. "Look at that," Lester whispered. "Would you look at that fiddle, like for a giant. Who would ever play such a thing? How could anybody get it on their shoulder? It looks too heavy—"

"You play it standing up like that, Lester. Shhhh." I drew closer. Even if he played it standing up, that little boy was awful small.

The next picture was of a family with three children. The mother had her sewing machine standing off to the side, and her two boys had on identical checkered shirts. On the mother's lap was a fat-faced baby in a long white dress.

"Would you look at that, Louisa. I bet they're twins. Look. They look exactly alike. I never saw twins before, did you, Louisa? Did you ever see twins in your life?"

"Lester, be quiet, would you? How can I look at these with you blabbering every minute?" I went on to the next picture, and the next, each one like the others, with the soddy behind a group of serious-looking people—children, parents, workers—but each picture was different, too. Special. There were horses with their bones nearly poking through their hides, soddies with bells on the roofs, pumps at the doors, skinny cottonwoods like Momma's displayed proudly as if they were members of the family.

"Louisa! Come here!" Lester was staring intently at one photograph with his nose almost touching it. "I think these are slaves. Come here. Tell me if these are slaves."

Momma was there beside me then, and we walked over to Lester together, and the three of us peered at the picture.

"My, my," Momma said. "Those are freed slaves, Lester. Come to settle in Nebraska and start a new life just like everybody else."

I had never seen real slaves before—or freed ones, either, for that matter. I held very still, wishing the picture were bigger. It was a family of eight people, with a windmill behind their soddy, and three horses and a fine wagon, and the man looked proud. His arms were crossed over his chest, and he was the only one looking directly out of the picture, right at us. Next to him were two small boys with shaven heads.

"Well, look at this," whooped Lester behind us. "If it isn't the old Whitfields!"

Momma laughed. "Lester! Keep your voice down."

We went to stand next to him, and I couldn't believe it. The Whitfields. People I actually knew and could recognize. There was Pru Whitfield, smug as you please, with a big old book in her lap, her Bible, no doubt—don't need no other, she'd say—and next to her was Carney Whitfield, looking strangely handsome when I knew he wasn't, with his hat on his knee and his wide suspenders outlining his broad chest. In the background was Paulie, holding the reins of their horse. I wondered how they ever got him to stand still long enough to be photographed. Probably bribed him, or held a gun to his head, that's what. You could tell by just looking that he'd never amount to much.

"Oh, look, children." It was Momma's soft voice, almost whispered. Her fingers were to her lips, and her eyes glistened. "It's us," she said. Lester and I went and stood on either side of her.

I'll tell you, I thought—well, I don't know *what* I thought, but I didn't expect to see such a mean little face on me. It would have really worried me, except Momma started laughing. "Oh, Louisa, that face! You are much prettier than that! See what a frown can do to you?" She placed her hand on my shoulder. I was well willing to believe I didn't look like *that* all the time. That it was just my serious face.

Actually, no one else in the photoprint was grinning from ear to ear, either. Poppa was looking down at Momma. He looked like himself, hard-working and capable, but I don't know, even looking at that picture I could tell he was anxious to get back to work. Momma looked serious, too, but very soft and gentle-looking. Suddenly I realized she didn't look at all like a walnut. I glanced up at her, standing there beside me, and I saw a faint glow on her cheeks, and a shininess and brightness to her dark eyes. My momma was truly a beautiful lady. I knew it that very moment, and I've always thought so to this very day. Not beautiful, maybe, like Mrs. Berryman had been, but beautiful in a way that made me feel good inside. Made me know how much I loved her. I slid my arm around her waist.

Next to Momma in the photoprint was Mrs. Berryman, captured and preserved for all time. I had forgotten exactly how her face looked, but not her hair and the way it had been when she first came, or the pretty way she smelled that day when she saw her soddy for the first time. Now, in the picture, I noticed she had the look of someone about to stand up and kick over her chair. Maybe I was just reading into things, but I felt a little frightened to see her there, still on the prairie, in her fading dress, with the swell of a baby beneath her dress.

"There you are, Lester," Momma said, pointing to the shadow of the soddy doorway, where there was a foot on the sill and a small hand pressed against the door.

"Well, look at that. . . ." he whispered.

"Fine likeness of you, Lester," I taunted.

"You better watch yourself, prairie dog," he threatened.

"Oh, hush, both of you," Momma said, and she held us close for just the smallest instant before she let us run free.

That evening it was time for the speeches and recitations. Momma had laid down the law about Lester—that's what Poppa had called it. Lester would not be forced to recite or read that year, so he was a bit like a pony let loose in a fresh pasture. There was an easiness about him that couldn't be riled, as if something inside had caught up with him.

But *I* still wanted to recite that poem Emmeline had first recited to me many months ago. Maybe it was a kind of thank-you to her, or maybe just a small sign to everyone else, telling them that a lady had come to Nebraska once and died, but that first she had taught me some poems and read me some books.

When everyone was gathered in the tent, and it was my turn to recite, I jumped up on the platform, faced that crowd who never even knew Emmeline, or cared much about her one way or the other, and suddenly I wasn't so sure about what I had decided to do. All those strangers' faces were turned up to me like sunflowers to the sun. My knees turned to water, and I was glad I had memorized the words because my hands were trembling and I had to grip them behind my back to keep them from embarrassing me.

Everyone waited, and it was quiet. I knew I had to begin.

" 'The Eagle: A Fragment,' " I said, surprised by my own voice, coming from I didn't know where, deep inside me. "By Tennyson." Several heads turned toward each other, a whisper or two. I cleared my throat.

> *"He clasps the crag with crooked hands;*
> *Close to the sun in lonely lands,*
> *Ring'd with the azure world, he stands.*
> *The wrinkled sea beneath him crawls;*
> *He watches from his . . . his . . ."*

I suddenly had no idea at all why I was up in front of all those people. I couldn't have told you my name at that moment. It seemed as if my mind had gone white-blank dead. None of the faces was familiar. I could have been peering into a chicken coop for all the difference it made. Nothing.

"His mountain walls!" someone shouted at me. Lester was standing up, his hands cupped around his mouth. I recognized him.

"His mountain walls," I repeated numbly.

I saw Momma, her fingers touched to her lips, waiting, waiting, and Poppa, his face apple-red from keeping in a smile. I smiled at him.

"And then like the thunderbolt he falls."

The people in the seats applauded and laughed, the terrible silence broken and over. I jumped down and ran back to my seat. Some old lady reached out and touched my arm with cool, dry fingers. "Very good," she said. "Good Tennyson, Louisa Downing."

The ride home was long, and Lester and me bedded down in the back of the wagon and watched the stars appear like great smudges of light, millions and millions of sparks, clouds upon clouds of stars, and the Milky Way arched above us like a bridge. There was a crescent moon on the horizon guiding us home. We lay side by side looking up into it.

I knew the celebration would be a memory of mine now, and I mulled it around in my mind like I would suck on a hard cherry candy ball, making it last and last. I especially wanted to remember Mr. Butcher's photoprint exhibit and the feeling I had when I saw the picture of all of us.

"You mad I didn't recite something?" Lester was talking to me.

"Nah. That's all right. You helped me, didn't you?"

"How come you're not mad at me? I thought you were going to be mad at me for not reading a poem or something."

"Nah."

A cool breeze passed over the wagon in a long sigh.

"Why's that?"

"Why's what, Lester?" He was starting to be annoying.

"Why'd you stop being mad?"

"I don't know." The stars seemed like a blessing. Nothing mattered at that moment except that I was with my momma and poppa and Lester, and we were traveling along in our wagon. "You'll do something in time. When you're ready. No use forcing a sunflower to bloom, or a calf to give milk. The sun comes up when the sun comes up. In time, Lester. You got time."

"Yes, but—"

"Lester." I leaned up on my elbow and peered at him.

"What?"

"You talk too much."

In the darkness, I heard him smile.